QUIET UNTIL

the

THAW

ALSO BY ALEXANDRA FULLER

Leaving Before the Rains Come
Fallings
Cocktail Hour Under the Tree of Forgetfulness
The Legend of Colton H. Bryant
Scribbling the Cat
Don't Let's Go to the Dogs Tonight

QUIET UNTIL

the

THAW

ALEXANDRA FULLER

PENGUIN PRESS
NEW YORK
2017

PENGUIN PRESS
An imprint of Penguin Random House LLC
375 Hudson Street
New York, New York 10014
penguin.com

"Quiet Until the Thaw" from *The Wishing Bone Cycle: Narrative Poems
from the Swampy Cree Indians*, gathered and translated by Howard A.
Norman (Stonehill Publishing, 1976).
Reprinted by permission of Howard A. Norman.

LIBRARY OF CONGRESS CATALOGING-IN-PUBLICATION DATA

Names: Fuller, Alexandra, 1969– author.
Title: Quiet until the thaw : a novel / Alexandra Fuller.
Description: New York : Penguin Press, 2017
Identifiers: LCCN 2016056759 (print) | LCCN 2017001457 (ebook) |
ISBN 9780735223349 (hardcover) | ISBN 9780735223356 (ebook) |
ISBN 9780735225145 (international edition)
Subjects: LCSH: Lakota Indians—Social life and customs—Fiction. |
Indians of North America—Fiction. | Domestic fiction. | BISAC:
FICTION / Literary. | FICTION / Historical.
Classification: LCC PS3606.U49 Q54 2017 (print) | LCC PS3606.U49
(ebook) |
DDC 813/.6—dc23
LC record available at https://lccn.loc.gov/2016056759

Printed in the United States of America
1 3 5 7 9 10 8 6 4 2

Designed by Amanda Dewey

T.D.F.

1940–2015

Nunc dimittis servum tuum, Domine,

secundum verbum tuum in pace

Life is a circle and we as common people are created to stand within it and not on it. I am not just of the past but I am the past. I am here. I am now and I will be for tomorrow.

—*Oglala Lakota maxim*

There are only two or three human stories, and they go on repeating themselves as fiercely as if they had never happened before.

—*Willa Cather*, O Pioneers

Quiet Until the Thaw

Her name tells of how
it was with her.

The truth is, she did not speak
in winter.
Everybody learned not to
ask her questions in winter,
once this was known about her.

The first winter this happened
we looked in her mouth to see
if something was frozen. Her tongue
maybe, or something else in there.

But after the thaw she spoke again
and told us it was fine for her that way.

So each spring we
looked forward to that.

*—Swampy Cree narrative naming poem**

---
* Translation from *The Wishing Bone Cycle*, by Howard A. Norman

All persons, living and dead, are purely coincidental.

—Kurt Vonnegut, *Timequake*

Part

ONE

Quiet Until the Thaw

They say Rick Overlooking Horse didn't talk much.

Actually, it was a little more than that. From the start, even for an Indian, his silence was bordering on worrying. For example, in his fourth spring, when You Choose Watson shot him in the leg with an arrow, he didn't go wailing to his grandmother like any normal kid. He turned his back on his Rez cousin's mocking laughter and limped away with the arrow still in his leg, down the hill toward the third in a row of tar-paper lean-tos on what is now Second Street in Manderson village. Then he stood in the kitchen, silent as ever, staring at his Closest Immediate Relation.

Mina Overlooking Horse, accustomed to her grandson's silence, took a long time to look up from the backseat of the 1935 Ford coupe that had served as her sofa since it had been torn from its crumpled mother chassis in a ditch outside

Chadron, Nebraska. Then she noticed the dark, viscous pool spreading on the earth floor beneath Rick Overlooking Horse's feet, and the arrow juddering from his leg. "Ayeee! You're making a mess of everything!" she said.

But Rick Overlooking Horse just blinked and stared at the dirt on which he was standing. Maybe he was wondering why You Choose had just shot him in the leg with an arrow. Or maybe he was wondering how he could mess everything up any worse than it already was. But no one would ever know what he was thinking about this, or much of anything else, because the child wouldn't talk.

It was like that Swampy Cree Indian poem, "Quiet Until the Thaw," as if his tongue must be frozen. Eventually, his grandmother and some of his More Concerned Immediate Relations thought to look in his mouth to make sure. But nope, everything was all defrosted and accounted for. Rick Overlooking Horse was simply a child, and then a man, of shockingly few words.

The Eternal Nature of Everything, as Described by Mina Overlooking Horse

By the time Rick Overlooking Horse was fixing to enter his second decade, he had uttered, all told, about enough words to fill a pamphlet from the Rezurrection Ministry outfit based out of Dallas, Texas. And those pamphlets were exceedingly short, designed as they were by little ladies with big hair for heathen Indians who had been out in the sun too long, so to speak.

Although to be fair, the little ladies were just doing their Christian bit. And to be accurate, some of them were very far from what you might describe as little. Plus, this was back in the early 1950s, which was a confusing time for a lot of people, particularly for people who counted on time being linear, one thing following another, one foot in front of the other, one breath after the other, from cradle to grave, accounting for all the time between birth and death, but accounting for none of the time between death and birth.

Mina made an attempt to get that confusion squared away early and often. "They say you've been here from the very start, and you'll be here to the very end," she told Rick Overlooking Horse when he was just nine years old. "Every last drop of you and everything around you. Nothing has ever been taken away. Nothing will ever be added." Then she sighed as if the very idea exhausted and perhaps saddened her. "Ayeee, they say that's true for you, it's true for You Choose, and it's true for me. Yep, it's true for the whole steaming, rotten lot of us." Mina let this sink in for a moment. "Like that breath you just took. In the beginning, a dinosaur breathed that breath. Then a tree. Then an ant. Then you, now me. And maybe it'll be You Choose next. Or maybe that breath will sink to the bottom of the ocean for one of those blind, ugly fish. Or maybe it will be someone's dying breath. You see? They say you just borrowed that breath. It wasn't yours to begin with and it won't be yours to end with."

Rick Overlooking Horse's
Tiny, Blown Mind

Nine-year-old Rick Overlooking Horse gave this a lot of thought, and his mind did what all minds have done since time immemorial while dealing with such a boundless, mysterious, obdurate idea. It blew up. Quite literally, it stopped working the way most people's minds work and it started off on its own kick. And that made Rick Overlooking Horse sleepless and also exalted. It was like angels should have been hovering in the clouds above his head, singing a chorus of sweet surrender. It was like his mind should have been able to trip heavenward on shafts of sunlight. It was like *that*.

Rick Overlooking Horse tried to come to some resolution about why he had chosen to be born now, at this time. He felt he needed some certainty, something that would make him feel less vulnerable, less miraculous, less unlikely. But in the end, he could not comprehensively solve a single thing about the reasons for his existence. All his answers opened trapdoors to further questions and those in turn revealed yet more trapdoors that slapped open to yet more unanswered questions.

Rick Overlooking Horse concluded that even half believing that you might be part of an incomprehensible, infinite, celestial phenomenon does not necessarily help a person figure out what to do with the bit of more or less graspable earthly life he or she has been given. For a start, he reasoned, a lot of what you do with your life depends on the body you find yourself in. To be born at this time, in this place, a more or less whole and healthy human being, for example, surely brings with it different complications and obligations than being born a more or less whole and healthy nematode more or less any time or place, let's just say.

"So, here I am," Rick Overlooking Horse thought, "and here it is: My life, as a human being. What are my choices?"

Well, Mina would argue that just for starters, being born into this world, in this time, was one choice. "You could have chosen not to be born now." She says this to You Choose whenever he winds himself up to whining pitch, which is often. "You could have been born when you had a chance to hunt buffalo, and live the way of All Our Ancestors. Yeah, and don't look at me like that, little Tapeworm. You ain't my doing. You're *your* doing."

Although to be fair to the choosers, Rick Overlooking Horse figured, perhaps almost all choices are mostly illusion given that almost all people seemed to be in a prison of their own making: Mina Overlooking Horse in a prison of resentment; You Choose Watson in a prison of need; some of the More Concerned Immediate Relations in a prison of fear, despair, and/or anger.

And for certain almost all people are in a prison of someone else's making. The way Rick Overlooking Horse saw it, one go-around, for example, a person might be a Oglala Lakota Oyate with the whole, high plains of buffalo to hunt. Next go-around, he's a Red Nigger orphan stuck with cornmeal, commodity cheese and beans, and Mina Overlooking Horse for a caretaker. Was that your choice, really?

Mina Overlooking
Horse's Winter Count

Waníyetu. Meaning, from first snowfall to first snowfall.
Wówapi. Meaning, flat surface.

Waníyetu wówapi. Meaning, Winter Count.

The year she got the boys, Mina Overlooking Horse drew two round bundles with wide-open mouths that represented the boys, and a bigger stick figure with a straight-across mouth that represented her. She wrote the number **216**, and underneath it, the number **12**. Then she drew a line under that, and wrote **204**. Every Winter Count after that, the stick figures of the children grew taller and thinner, and the stick figure that represented her grew shorter and fatter. And every year, Mina Overlooking Horse subtracted another 12 months from her sentence as reluctant caretaker.

192, 180, 168, 156

Winter Count after Winter Count.

Winter Count after Winter Countdown.

"Oh, take them from me," Mina Overlooking Horse had prayed the words aloud one night after both boys had eaten larkspur flowers and spent two days vomiting and sweating and twitching. And then she had slapped her hand over her mouth and held her breath because someone had once told her that in order to think, you had to get oxygen to the brain, and Mina Overlooking Horse did not want to think about what it was she had just said, or why.

Then, in 1952, when they were eight, and Mina Overlooking Horse's Winter Count was down by **96**, the boys were shipped off to Fort Carmichael Indian Boarding School in Oklahoma, where the matron shaved their heads, threw away their beads, and burned their blankets. The following year, Mina Overlooking Horse's stick-figure boys looked willow thin, and hollow eyed. The figure that represented her had its arms stretched out, as if reaching for someone or perhaps pushing someone away.

You Choose Watson and the
Sugar Debacle of 1962

It's never been so easy for a Lakota boy to worm his way out of his military responsibilities. For a start, most Indians are in boarding school, already roped, as it were, when their enlistment papers come. And for another thing, it's not as if an Indian boy has a hope of getting a legal deferment to complete his education at Yale or a family-friend doctor who can declare the boy flat-footed or cross-eyed or afflicted with bone spurs and therefore unfit for military service. In fact, you might say the United States Army has its fingers on an Indian boy's shoulders before the ink on his U.S. government-issued Certificate of Degree of Indian Blood is even dry.

But when his notice came to report for a physical as a preliminary to being drafted into the U.S. armed forces, You

Choose consumed so much sugar—three stolen one-pound bags—that he felt drunk for two days and light-headed for a week. It was sheer genius, honestly.

"You Choose Watson," the recruitment officer said. "Is that a real name?"

You Choose was having a hard time with his vision. He put a hand over one eye, and that seemed to help narrow the recruitment officer down to a single figure.

"Is that a real name?" the recruitment officer asked again.

"Yeah," You Choose Watson said, swallowing. Nausea and mild sweats were also part of his current infliction.

The recruitment officer said, "Stand up straight, boy."

You Choose Watson hiccupped, and then burped.

But he didn't get shipped out to Southeast Asia.

Mina Overlooking Horse stared at the piece of paper from the U.S. Army Recruiting Command, Rapid City, South Dakota. She could not read well, but she could read well enough to see that it declared You Choose Watson unfit for military service on account of his diabetes.

"Your what?" she said.

Then she looked at the birch bark wall in which she had made her Winter Count every year for eighteen years until, this year, she had been finally able to write the number *0* and she said, "I didn't know him well, but I believe your father would have been real proud of you."

The Etymology of the Name "You Choose Watson"

Back then, winters were something to endure. A person had to be deliberate, watch her step, remember that a view can shrink into the white tunnel in front of your nose. Life-snatching winds, entombing ice, snow amassing like a sudden land feature, hands made raw with cold.

But when spring arrived, the memory of winter faded like a woman's memory of childbirth. Whatever had just happened, life was in front of her now, bursting and fresh and relentless and hungry, and she couldn't stay holed up remembering that only a month earlier, the weather had seemed intent on murder.

Even so, no one who lived through it would ever forget the winter of 1944.

All anyone could think about was the cold, and how to

get out of it. The wind drove snow into the roads and sheared everything to ice. For months there appeared to be no difference between earth and sky, everything looked the same silver-grey. Inside the lean-tos and teepees across the Rez, Indians bent over fires, inhaling so much smoke their lungs filled with fluid and their feet and hands swelled from lack of motion. Dogs froze solid to the edges of the road, becoming more white mounds in a landscape of other white mounds.

Among the Indians sheltering on the Rez from the hungry wind that winter was a Cowboy who went under the name of Elijah Watson. Well, I say Cowboy, but he wasn't much of that. All hat and no cattle, as they say. Not afraid to stand at stud though, if you know what I mean. In fact, he'd run himself out of six states already on that account. Minnesota, Missouri, Oklahoma, Nebraska, Kansas, and North Dakota. Now he was just waiting for the weather to lighten up, and he'd be adding South Dakota to the list.

In this way, You Choose Watson was born half Cowboy, half Indian, and—as Mina liked to say afterward—the missing half of each. Which is to say the boy was born with an itinerant Cowboy as a father and a sore-hearted Indian girl as a mother.

The sore-hearted Indian girl stared down at the baby offered up for her inspection by Mina Overlooking Horse, who was for much of her life the unofficial, not to say unwilling, midwife of the Lakota Oglala Sioux Nation.

Mina said, "Well?"

The Indian looked at Mina, generations of defeat in her eyes.

"Well?" Mina said again.

The Indian looked at the Cowboy. "What should we call him?" she asked.

Elijah Watson had been trying, with mixed results, to absent himself mentally from the scene for some time and, having finally succeeded to some degree, he was not about to get pulled back into the room by the presence of a squalling kid. He shrugged. "I don't know. You choose," he said.

"You Choose," the sore-hearted Indian whispered, and sank against the greasy towel beneath her head. She gave a filleted smile and nodded. "You Choose," she said again. "Yeah, that's a good name for this child."

A Month After You Choose
Watson Was Born

They say trouble gets lonely pretty easily, and that is why it always comes in threes, or pairs at least. So it was no surprise when a month after finding herself the unwilling recipient of the infant You Choose Watson—"Such a rotten baby," she used to say—Mina's own recently widowed daughter-in-law gave birth to a son.

February 4, 1944. You can't say the winter had let up any. Still, birth doesn't wait for the conditions to improve, so here was Rick Overlooking Horse quietly slipping into the world, as if hoping the world wouldn't notice, which it didn't, incidentally. Even his own mother turned her face to the wall when Mina presented the baby to her. "He looks quiet, at least," Mina said, in what she hoped were encouraging tones.

The mother wept silently.

Mina Overlooking Horse sighed and sat down on the backseat of the 1935 Ford coupe and thought about how much she would like someone to bring her a cigarette or a cup of coffee, or both. She stared at the freshly delivered infant in the basket at her feet. In another basket by the fire, You Choose Watson was beginning to whimper. In a few minutes, he'd have wound himself up into a state and he'd be hollering.

She said, "Well, I guess someone's got to do it."

She sighed again, heaved herself to her feet, hands on knees, and fetched up You Choose Watson. She put him to her withered breast.

"This one sucks like a bicycle pump," she complained. "The White ones always do." She closed her eyes and sank back against the wall. Then she said, "For the love of mercy, I'll take a cigarette now. Does anyone have a cigarette?"

She was forty years old and she had given suck to at least one child—only three of them her own—every year for the last twenty-four years.

All Are Related,
Related to All

M itakuye Oyasin. Meaning, All My Relations.

Or, Everything is related to the existence of all my Lakota relatives.

Meaning, this counts out the White Man; or, to be more precise, White Man thinking.

Meaning, everything is connected in a web so complicated and invisible, it takes being born Indian to understand the intricacies of kinship.

Skinship, the youth say.

Every Immediate and Distant Relation freaked out about the possibility of incest, especially since everyone has been rounded up like cattle, corralled on reservations, and given Certificates of Degree of Indian Blood.

Under the laws and bylaws of the U. S Department of the

Interior, there is no choice for Indians: They must either watch themselves disappear drop of blood by drop of blood, or they must marry their cousins, which is the same as driving a stake through the heart of a Lakota.

The English and White Settler Americans, on the other hand, appear to have no taboo against incest. Even among the so-called leaders of the White Man, cousins regularly marry one another, generation after generation, more or less openly fucking their daughters, nieces, and granddaughters, eventually creating a class of chinless, insecure, wig-wearing golfers.

It takes an Indian amount of knowing to understand that rocks are grandfathers, plants are nations.

It takes an Indian amount of holiness to understand that thunderclouds are not only beings, but Higher Beings.

You've got to lose all fear of loss to know the world like an Indian, All My Relations.

You've got to be tuned in like a bat to know what messages the Great Spirit brings, and to trust your knowing enough to act on that knowledge.

The (Other) Red Scare(s)

Rick Overlooking Horse was born under a waxing gibbous moon.

He was born during the Month of Wolves.

He was born in the Season of Hunger.

He was born when Trees Crack from the Cold.

He was born under the sign of Aquarius.

He was born during the Second Red Scare, and on the same day as the formation of the Motion Picture Alliance for the Preservation of American Ideals in Los Angeles, California, of which Walt Disney was a founding member.

Is it the stars under which we are born that will affect the course of our lives? Or is it everything else that was in the process of being born on the day of our births that will affect the course of our lives?

If we believe it to be the former, we risk sounding untethered.

If we believe it to be the latter, we risk sounding unhinged.

If we understand it at all, we are struck speechless with terror, and wonder.

But a lot of people are likely to believe nothing, and understand little.

For example, all people with their minds set on power must forget how everything repeats and repeats and repeats itself. They must forget how empires rise and fall; civilizations flourish and collapse.

It has always been this way, and yet people with their minds set on power act as if they are not part of an undeniable, inevitable, inescapable cycle. They deny the infinite ways in which they are connected to everything else.

People with their minds set on power act as if it can't happen again, whatever it was.

The Lakota act in the knowledge that certainly it will happen again, whatever it is.

Meantime, Names for a Red Man, and Why He Doesn't Care

Diesel," the other soldiers in Rick Overlooking Horse's unit called him, short for "Diesel Engine," long for Injun. Or "Hatch," short for Hatchet Packer. Or "Feather Nigger," "Red Nigger," "Hey, Wagon Burner," they said. "All good-natured josh," they swore. "No offence," they insisted. Although the Red Man's silence was a bit disturbing, like maybe he knew something they didn't.

Which it turned out, of course, he did.

Because before Indian boarding school swallowed them up, Mina Overlooking Horse taught the boys this way: Some nights, when she'd smoked Wahupta, and was feeling tender with them as they lay on blankets at the foot of her bed in the tar-paper lean-to, she told them the story of the Battle of the

Greasy Grass, speaking softly into the wind-blown dark. Usually, there would be a candle casting jumping, spooky shadows against the yellow wall and the world seemed very small then, and mysterious.

"The morning of the battle was cool, because it was June and summer was still warming itself up," she would always start this way. "The warriors awoke early and rode far from the village, away from the women and children. They took only the bravest horses into battle." And so Mina Overlooking Horse talked on and on into the night, pausing only to smoke more Wahupta. "And they brought with them only what they would be prepared to lose. In other words, prairie chickens, they brought their lives. Because they knew they were fighting for everything that they were, everything that they had been, and for everything that you are."

In this way, the story of the Battle of the Greasy Grass, commonly known as Custer's Last Stand, also known as the Battle of the Little Bighorn, became the tapestry of Rick Overlooking Horse's young imagination. He hugged himself under his blanket and made pictures out of Mina Overlooking Horse's words. He knew exactly how dew would be bowing the heads of the grass, he knew the way the horses would smell salty and warm, he thought of how everything must have been sharp and clear in the minds of the warriors. "The first day, the battle continued until dark," Mina Overlooking Horse would say, "and it began again at first light."

And although Rick Overlooking Horse and You Choose

Watson knew word for word how the story would end, they always made sure that they stayed awake to hear it because the end was their favorite part. "During his Sundance, Sitting Bull had had a vision of soldiers falling into his camp like grasshoppers from the sky, and so it came to be. And they say one day it will be again. They say one day the lights will go out, and the White Man will succumb to the dark, but that we will remain since we are not afraid when the sun sets. Like fox, raven, wolf, and vulture, we are masters of the night. That is what they say."

A Quick Note on the
Word "Indian"

In the English dictionary, the most oft-cited authority is the Holy Bible, and the most oft-cited author is Shakespeare. It's a good start, but it's a very narrow perspective, if you think about it, and it also explains some stuff. For example, some people say Christopher Columbus described the first Indians he encountered in the so-called New World as "una gente in Dios."

Meaning, a People in God.

There's no actual proof Christopher Columbus had God or God's People in mind when he bumped into Haiti on December 4, 1492, and accidentally introduced what happened next to two continents.

Maybe, like some people say, he thought he'd blundered into India instead of Hispaniola. And it is possible that as far as he was concerned, brown people = Indian. Although it's nicer to imagine he meant the other thing.

In Dios.

Except doesn't it then make what happens next worse? A people in God, gone.

Because whatever else you can say about the man, Christopher Columbus's visit did not leave the Antilles better than when he found it, the most beautiful land he'd ever seen, he wrote in his diary, of present day Haiti.

Crumpled mountains in the clouds, dense with towering hardwood forests and cut through with tumbling, crystal-clear rivers. Fertile plains surrounded by water on all sides, the sea blue and green as jewels in a perpetual spring, replete with fish, guarded by coral reefs. And all the creatures of the fertile valleys—the solendons and shrews and hutias—dappled and blending among the grasses, sheltering beneath the buttressed roots of the great Ceiba tree, feasting off the flesh of one another so that nothing lived too long, but most things didn't live too short either.

All that, plundered and lost.

Although time being what it is, the playground of monsters and madmen is also the residence of lovers and poets.

The light is always equal to the dark.

Time being what it is, it always was.

Victor Charlie and
the Indian

There had been signs, warnings, and portents, and eventually Rick Overlooking Horse pointed them out: The smell of fresh human urine in the grass beside the path; the way birds half a mile ahead were clattering into the sky and circling above the jungle, visible through the occasional chink in the foliage; crimped branches and bruised leaves.

To say nothing of the fact, there was no one around or at least no one anyone could see. This many days into the patrol they should have seen villagers, some kids, a couple of farmers, somebody, anybody, by now. But there wasn't even fresh spoor to go with the smell of fresh urine.

It is true that ghosts don't leave footprints, but neither do they digest.

And while it is easy enough to cover your tracks, it is

nearly impossible to cover up the scent of urine, especially urine that is vinegary with stress and dehydration.

A flexible, wild mind will register the misconnections.

It was clear.

Or at least it was clear to Rick Overlooking Horse. Victor Charlie was using an old Indian technique. Lure the enemy deep into unfamiliar territory, days away from backup, and then unleash the full force of your unconventional, unexpected fury on them. A disorientated, overladen, homesick nine-man rifle squad didn't stand a chance against even one deft, well-adapted gook.

Rick Overlooking Horse said, "It ain't natural."

"It ain't natural, *sir*," Staff Sergeant Urbaniak said. Then he said, "What ain't natural?"

Rick Overlooking Horse said, "None of it."

"Shee-it," Staff Sergeant Urbaniak said, employing the Redneck accent that in no way, could it be accused, came easily to him. "None of it, *sir*. What do you mean, 'None of it'?"

But Rick Overlooking Horse had never seen the point of saying most things once, let alone anything twice. Also he understood that Staff Sergeant Urbaniak wasn't in a hearing kind of mood. He was a doughy Polack from the Bay Area with something to prove, even if it was just the fact that not every male in his graduating class was a draft-dodging, pot-smoking beatnik.

Staff Sergeant Urbaniak said, "You know something,

Diesel? You're just jittery. You've got to stay calm and cool. I thought you people were supposed to be good at that."

The two men stood in a small, sunlit clearing, the exchange of their words hanging between them. Suddenly Rick Overlooking Horse made a grunt like a horse getting the wind kicked out of it. He hauled back and with all his strength he knocked Staff Sergeant Urbaniak as far as he could in the direction of the jungle. Then he threw his pack twelve feet into the jungle in the other direction and dove after it.

"What the hell!" Staff Sergeant Urbaniak stood up, wiped the mud off his face, and scrambled back into the clearing. "Oh, fuck, now you've got it comin'." He turned to face the rest of his rifle squad, grinning. "Diesel's gone dinky cow, boys." Then he shook his finger into the thicket where Rick Overlooking Horse lay out of sight, curled up like a punctuation mark between what was happening now, and what would happen next. "Get your yeller-bellied, dumb, fucking, red-wop ass up and outta there, and explain your conduct, or you'll find yourself on the receiving end of . . ."

Dog Tags Are Forever

But no one ever found out what Rick Overlooking Horse was about to be on the receiving end of.

When they got to him, they found the Indian's dog tags had seared into his chest, soldered there by the force of the fire that had hit his squad, exploding the trees around them and scattering their clothes and flesh and bones. But the words and number were still visible, barely. "Overlooking Horse. Rick. 720939846. Mina Overlooking Horse. Manderson Pine Ridge, South Dakota."

They say hearing is the last sense to go, that it's important to keep speaking to the dying. But it is not possible to hear a human voice over a helicopter, or a cargo plane, or a W200 Dodge Power Wagon ambulance. Plus, not to put too fine a point on it, it was clear the Indian was soon to be a corpse. It might be that the paramedics—if they were thinking at all—were of the opinion that if Rick Overlooking Horse could hear anything from this world, it wouldn't be too long before he couldn't.

Unless There's Extreme, Unforeseen Heat

The last anyone saw of Staff Sergeant Lucas "Lucky Luke" Urbaniak, he was a pink mist drifting down from the sky. His dog tags were never recovered. They too were vaporized. No one saw that coming. Not Staff Sergeant Urbaniak, not the dog-whistling four-star generals in the U.S. Army, not even the Battle Creek Dog Tag Company out of Tulsa, Oklahoma.

But then, who could have predicted friendly fire in such an unfriendly space? Who could have anticipated the U.S. brown-water navy deploying an ignited napalm mixture from a riverboat-mounted flamethrower toward a confirmed target, without realizing, oh, dear God, surely without realizing exactly what they were doing? Who could come up with a dog tag that could withstand a temperature of 2,200 degrees Fahrenheit?

They say when Country Joe and the Fish played the "Fixin' to Die Rag" at Woodstock, Joe had his old schoolmate on his mind, but who knows for sure? "There's about three hundred thousand of you fuckers out there," Country Joe yelled at the soggy crowd. "I want you to start singin'. Come on!"

Who knows for sure who was the more deluded? The hawkish, something-to-prove Polack Staff Sergeant Urbaniak who thought he'd be unscathed and home by Christmas, or the angry-as-hell peacenik leader of a psychedelic rock band who thought he could stop a war if enough people sang along with him.

Thanatopsis

You'll hear people from the Bureau of Indian Affairs say Indians sleep all day. Show up any time, even during so-called working hours, they'll tell you, and you'll find all the kids running wild in the hills with a pack of Rez dogs, and all the adults passed out. It's never occurred to anyone to suppose the kids and the dogs are running for their lives and the adults are not asleep so much as playing possum. Tonic immobility, the scientists would say. Thanatopsis.

So when the White Men in U.S. Army uniforms arrived at the earthen-floored, tar-paper lean-to in Manderson village and knocked on the door and peered this way and that at the ancient-household-appliance-strewn yard for signs of human life, Mina Overlooking Horse stayed catatonic seeming beneath her quilts. She heard them head over to the neighbor's place, but they were playing dead too. She waited until she heard the White Men leave and then she got up and lit a fire. She burned enough sage to choke a horse.

Mina Overlooking Horse never did open the telegram the White Men had left on her door. She didn't need to. Ill fate was a crafty hunter. You couldn't outwit, outrun, or out-downwind it. "Ayeee," Mina said. She lit a fire and burned the unopened envelope. Then she looked up and saw her old Winter Counts behind the woodstove, the little figures of the early years worn away to smudges. She took a piece of charcoal from the woodstove and scrubbed over the writing.

Then she wiped her hands on her knees and put the kettle on to boil. There was a scald mark on the roof, oily grey smoke in the air, and a fist-sized hole in the kettle before Mina realized there had been no water in it to start with, and now her kettle was soldered to the stove.

You Choose on
Turtle Island

Meantime, You Choose Watson headed north of the border, if you are the kind of person who believes in borders, which You Choose Watson claimed not to do. "There are no borders on Turtle Island," he proclaimed. "That never was the way of our people." Sometimes he told of being chased through the forests by dogs and men on horses, which was mostly a drama of his imagination. Make that, entirely a drama of his imagination, although it's true that once he woke up in an alleyway in Vancouver with a hangover. And another time he had an accident while attempting to shower in the sink in a men's washroom in a train station. So, it hadn't all been smooth sailing.

In a village in northern British Columbia, You Choose hired on with a crew, cleaning fishing rigs. Which was work, obviously. And smelly, difficult, unlovely work while it was at it. So when he heard about an Indian encampment in unceded territory, free for all natives interested in a traditional way of life, off the reserves, off the grid, off the beaten track, he was there like an arrow. "At home we have a saying," he said. "One man is a person, but many men are a people."

For a full summer, he grew out his hair, attended ceremonies, and avoided having to do much in the way of anything. He loved the company. "Brother," those northwestern Indians called him. He loved the damp, mild summer, nothing torrid and violent about that weather, not like the Rez. And he loved being the exotic Indian. He made up stories about getting into brawls with Cowboys, and oh, the Wild, Wild Western ways of sheriffs and buffaloes and Indian war ponies. And when he was called upon to do something he did not feel like doing, he came up with an easy out. "We have a saying back home," he said. "Water and wind wear away rock better than picks and axes."

He liked too the way those northwestern people spoke like they had until tomorrow to get the words out of their mouths. Also, they used inflection at the end of their sentences that made everything sound like a question. "Watson?" So that it wasn't too much of a stretch for You Choose to come up with the idea of altering the spelling of his name, perhaps the way it always should have been. "What Son," he said.

You Choose What Son.

There was a holy, mysterious ring to the name now that

You Choose liked. Spelled this new way, there was nothing jokey and cavalier about it, nothing careless and shameful. It was more like an invitation to bend your head in respectful wonder. And you didn't have to have Catholicism drummed into you by some damp-palmed, pedophilic priest at an Indian boarding school to extrapolate a messiah figure out of You Choose What Son. "We have a saying back home," he said. "You have to live yourself into a name, not name yourself into a life."

It should be noted here that a couple of women rolled their eyes. "Never heard so much treaty talk in my life," one muttered. "Hope he doesn't get too comfortable here."

Candlefish Forever

You Choose had never been so happy. Except for the food, which was an incessant diet of fatty candlefish, augmented with the odd tart berry. Holy buffalo, what those people wouldn't do with a candlefish couldn't be done. They smoked them, boiled them, baked them, poached them, charred them, and worst of all they ate them raw. Sometimes You Choose had dreams in which he was eating seared red meat; so vivid he woke up with the greasy-salty taste of stew in his mouth.

At the Northern Waters Café in a coastal village near the encampment, You Choose What Son found he could trade out five hours of kitchen work for a full meal and kitchen leftovers to take home. He preferred to work the Sunday morning shift, five until ten, before the after-church crowd came in. Then he'd linger over coffee, steak, eggs, and a fry-up of potatoes until he was fit to burst. "Good thing you came north, brother," the café's cook said one morning, throwing the Sunday paper down for You Choose What Son to see the headline: "**US Casualties in Vietnam Rise to 1,387.**"

The café's cook was from the Yukon with an attitude that You Choose didn't quite like and which he attributed to the matrilineal society from which she had come. She gave the impression of being impenetrable and unwavering, like she'd distilled all the parts of herself you might ordinarily consider personality into internal granite. She also spoke extra slowly, even for these people. So slowly it could be hard for a person to stay on track until the end of what she had to say, which, luckily for her listeners, was usually not more than a handful of words.

You Choose What Son shook his head and wiped his mouth. "Yeah," he said, "it was my warrior act of resistance not to participate in that criminal carnage."

"That so?" the cook said.

You Choose took a big gulp of coffee and wiped his mouth with the back of his hand. "Yeah, the White Man sending the Red Man and the Black Man to kill the Yellow Man. Where's the sense in that?"

"Where indeed?" the cook replied.

You Choose made a casual noise in his throat. In his mind, he was thinking it might be time to move on. Maybe the East Coast this time, he thought, with those New York

Mohawks. Maybe that was the next place for him. He'd heard the border was easy to cross there too, if you didn't mind getting your feet wet.

And it was a cheap place to live if you didn't mind the humid winters, the black mold, and the impregnable, stinging undergrowth. Plus, he'd heard the Mohawks were the tough-as-tomahawks, take-no-prisoner kind of Indians, and he was about ready for Indians with whom he could throw around some pent-up macho.

Thaté: Wind

Meantime, back in the VA hospital, Rick Overlooking Horse unhinged his mind from the impatience of waiting for anything to change, ever. He attached himself only to the consistency of the present, and to the inevitability of his pain. Pain, like a relentless spring wind, changeable and unremitting, sometimes blustering, sometimes softly pressing, but nonetheless constant.

He remembered this: When he was a small boy, he and You Choose Watson and Mina had spent a week at an underground Sundance Ceremony way out beyond Rockyford on the edge of the Mako Sica. These were the long decades in which the U.S. government officially outlawed all manifestations of Indian spirituality, so the Rez was thick with agents every summer seeking out anyone who might be preparing to partake in the Sacred Medicine of the talking tree.

All through Sundance, the heat gathered and gathered, as if harnessing itself for an onslaught. Grasshoppers crackled in the drying grass. Cicadas shrilled. The aspens shimmered lime green. Rick Overlooking Horse and You Choose ran barefoot among the Sundance participants. They played with the whelped puppies. They ran between the legs of the Indian war ponies. They watched the women preparing themselves for purification. They spied on the men preparing themselves to hear the messages of the talking tree.

Then, at noon on the day of the Sundance, the boys crept out from under the walls of the teepee where Mina had left them to sleep through the heat of the afternoon. They crawled on their bellies through the baking grass to the arbor. There they saw the men emerge from the purification lodge, sweating but dry eyed. They heard the elder celebrant chanting, his prayers rising with the heat. The leaves of the great cottonwood shook and trembled; its limbs hung about with bright bundles of tobacco.

The men offered themselves up to branches of the tree.

Or, you could say they offered themselves as living sacrifices to God.

You Choose saw blood, and vomited in the grass.

A raven that had been tumbling about above the arbor suddenly cried and dived out of the sky, its wings brushing the leaves of the cottonwood tree.

Rick Overlooking Horse took all this in, then he sank to his young knees and put his hands and forehead on the grass.

"I'm yours," he said. "Use me."

That night, after the ceremonial meal and after the men's wounds had been bathed in salt water by the herbalists, and after the leader of the ceremony had prayed, a storm rolled in across the plains. Clouds towered like celestial battleships in the west, lightning bulleted out of the sky, and thunder reverberated. Everyone retreated to shelter.

You Choose wept and had had to be put under blankets and held fast. But Rick Overlooking Horse felt only exhilaration. The wind crashed, and surged, and crashed, and surged, bowing the canvas of the teepee, and Rick Overlooking Horse smiled and curled himself around Mina's legs and for once she did not kick him away but instead tolerated his little body against her papery skin. Rick Overlooking Horse felt for You Choose Watson's hand and found it shaking.

For the first time, Rick Overlooking Horse understood that fear is what comes of trying to live more than one life at a time.

Time

The way Rick Overlooking Horse saw it, he could return to that teepee, to Mina's dry skin and You Choose Watson's clammy little hand any time he chose. Time was not stable. Time was like wind, or currents. It did not plod forward; it could flow backward, or spiral inward, or slide around on a plane. All Time was possible, all the time. The only skill needed was an ability to pilot the tides, the troughs and the dips.

How obvious it all was.

Rick Overlooking Horse laughed inwardly, sadly, the way you do when you realize how much suffering you have had to endure to know one true, obvious thing. It was as the priests had chanted morning and night in that terrible boarding school in Kansas: "Sicut erat in principio, et nunc, et semper, et in sæcula sæculorum."

As it was in the beginning, is now, was always, and ever will be.

Time, is all time is, and has been, and will be, forever and ever.

Mni: Water

A few months later, when it was apparent the Indian was, in fact, not only inexplicably alive but also miraculously awake, a doctor asked, "What's your name?"

It was not a complicated question. But the answer was longer than Rick Overlooking Horse was prepared to give.

"Hau," he managed. The syllable cost him nearly everything.

"Your name?" the doctor tried again, louder. "Who are you?"

His Certificate of Degree of Indian Blood said he was seven-eighths Lakota Oglala. They say the missing eighth belonged to an Irish Pony Express rider back in 1860 or 1861, and accounted for the freckles on Rick Overlooking Horse's nose and back.

Mina Overlooking Horse, his grandmother, was a direct descendent of Spotted Elk.

Nobody Overlooking Horse, his father, was crossed over.

His mother was also crossed over. Presumably in search of the man she loved.

"Who are you?" the doctor persisted. "Do you know who you are?"

Rick Overlooking Horse gestured the air with his hand. It felt shimmering, alive, vibrating with tiny particles like a thin soup, or broth, but drier.

"Do you understand what has happened?" the doctor said.

A fly buzzed against a window nearby. Wherever they were, it sounded hot to Rick Overlooking Horse. He wondered whose summer he was having.

The doctor fired off a list of questions.

"Who is the president of the United States?"

"Do you know what year this is?"

"Where are you?"

Rick Overlooking Horse thought of a summer storm. He thought of rain falling on the prairie. He pictured Little Wounded Knee Creek in full flood. He visualized the White River tumbling east. He turned himself into the Missouri and he poured himself into the Mississippi. Then he washed out into the Gulf of Mexico.

He knew no pain lasts forever. Either it will pass, or you will.

The trick, always, was to surrender.

Maka: Earth

When they took the bandages off, Rick Overlooking Horse was unsurprised to discover that his left eyelid had been sewn shut. Through his right eye things appeared gauzy at first, as if he were looking through a lens smeared with Vaseline. Light bulged and pulsed and pained. Rick Overlooking Horse closed his eye and sank back against the pillow. He wondered if he no longer belonged to his body, since the limbs that stretched beneath the sheets were wizened, wrinkled, and atrophied. They belonged to a dead man. They were not his.

Some days later, the nurse held up a mirror so that Rick Overlooking Horse could behold himself. But the mirror shook, as if he and the nurse were bouncing down a corrugated dirt road on the Rez in the back of a pickup truck. Rick Overlooking Horse saw shuddering fragments of a creature that appeared to belong not here, or there, but between earth, water, and sky, something amphibious, in other words.

The nurse mistook Rick Overlooking Horse's silence for something worse. "Oh, bless your ever-loving heart. I'm so sorry," she whispered. "I am so very, very sorry."

Phéta: Fire

The cover of *Life* magazine, October 30, 1964, showed America's greatest swimmer, Don Schollander, with four Olympic gold medals on his chest. He looked young and blond, staring with every confidence into the future as if he could already see his medals on display for the public at the Bank of America in downtown Lake Oswego, Oregon.

Inside the magazine, there was Pope Paul VI proclaiming twenty-two African saints. There was an advertisement for crochet granny dresses that might reasonably be expected to shock an actual grandmother. There was Martin Luther King Jr. winning the Nobel Peace Prize. And finally there was Billy Mills, the unknown long-shot American runner, winning the 10,000 meters.

The magazine was nearly a year out of date when the nurse showed it to Rick Overlooking Horse. She'd been saving it all these months for him because of the photo of Billy Mills, arms flung back, chest bursting through the ribbon, eyes closed, mouth torn in joy.

"Look, he's Indian too," the nurse said. "And a soldier." She read slowly, as if she weren't sure Rick Overlooking Horse could hear, or as if maybe she thought English were not his mother tongue. "A first lieutenant in the Marine Corps," she added.

Rick Overlooking Horse turned his head away.

"Did you know him?" the nurse asked. She took the Indian's hand and stroked it.

There's so much space on the Rez, and so little in between the space. There was so much that might end you before you had a proper chance to begin. There was so much against you.

Of course you ran in packs.

Until even your people could not save you.

Then, you ran alone.

"Yeah," Rick Overlooking Horse said. "We ran together."

"What a coincidence!" the nurse said. Her touch was fire to Rick Overlooking Horse. It was acid. It was a skinning. The nurse said, "Am I hurting you?"

Thaté, Again

Billy Mills was the fastest Indian in the world and even he couldn't outrun the officials from the Bureau of Indian Affairs when they came for him and for all the kids between the ages of six and twelve that boreal chorus frog-singing August afternoon in 1952. "When they come for you, run," the elders had said. By which they had meant, "Our power to protect you ends in that moment."

So there was Billy Mills and Rick Overlooking Horse and You Choose Watson and a whole, sweet, sweating mess of Indian kids running with a pack of Rez dogs like their lives depended on it, off roads, over the prairie, through gullies, darting this way and that, and the Bureau of Indian Affairs patrol cars bumping behind them. One of the officers had a bullhorn and was shouting something that got distorted in the hot prairie wind.

"We're here to help you! We're here to help you!"

Blood pounded in Rick Overlooking Horse's ears.

"We're here to scalp you!" he heard. "We're here to scalp you!"

They caught Billy Mills last of all, but they caught him still. You would have thought they could have let at least one little Indian get away. But, "Kill the Indian, Save the Man," was the official mission statement of the Bureau of Indian Affairs, and they took the first part of that mandate very seriously. They didn't save Billy Mills the Child either, but they forever ingrained in him the importance of running faster than you think your legs can spin and your lungs can pump.

"Look at Mills! Look at Mills!" Dick Bank screamed in Tokyo in 1964 for the entire television-watching, radio-listening world to hear. "Oh, my God, Mills is coming on!" He sounded so hysterical NBC fired him on the spot.

Italians/~~Indians~~
Cry Too

Before the Keep America Beautiful campaign that showed Chief Iron Eyes Cody shed a single tear when he saw the mess the White Man had made of the Earth, it was commonly believed by non-Indians that Indians didn't cry. Sure, in historical depictions they looked defeated, and slumped over on their war ponies. And if you paid attention to modern photographs they looked pretty binged out. But you never thought of Indians as sad per se. You thought of them as stoic.

Skipping lightly over the fact that Chief Iron Eyes Cody wasn't a real Indian at all, not Cherokee-Cree as he claimed—he was, in fact, of Italian descent—what it did show is that Indians were mostly whatever Other People needed them to be.

The fact is, even with just one eye, Rick Overlooking Horse cried tears like a river for Billy Mills, and not just tears of joy because that Indian had run like the wind and shown the world the power of his mind and the power of his body, but also because Rick Overlooking Horse knew Billy Mills had been through the literal definition of hell to earn those wings. I mean, what were the odds?

A half-breed orphan raised in poverty in the 1950s on the Pine Ridge Indian Reservation who nonetheless survived boarding school and got an athletic scholarship to the University of Kansas and who had once stood on the edge of a hotel window after a college track meet and considered his body in flight, or really in free fall, without wings, and somehow decided against it. "Can the dark one step out of the picture?" the photographer had asked that afternoon.

In the end, when he had won the gold medal and everyone wanted him for their hero, they couldn't put the dark one into enough pictures. They made movies about him, and wrote books, and built a community hall in Pine Ridge village in his honor. And they gave him a Lakota name, Makata Taka Hela, meaning, Respects the Earth. Which became inconvenient for the U.S. government trying their best to staunch the burgeoning environmental and peace-love-and-tolerance movements sweeping across the land. "Loves his Country," they decided was a better, more patriotic sounding translation of the phrase, more in keeping with their needs.

Mina Overlooking Horse Drinks Coffee as a Substitute for Having a Feeling

Rick Overlooking Horse returned to the Rez after a year and a half in the hospital. He had a shaved head and a black patch where his left eye had been. His skin had the stretched, shiny appearance of melted plastic. The freckles on his nose, passed down from the Irish Pony Express rider, had run into brown-purple ink stains across his cheeks.

Mina said, "Ayeee, is that you? But oh, they made a mess of you." She wheezed a little. "They came, you know, with a telegram. But well, I never did open it. Nothin' I could do about it anyway, except pray, I guess. Although if you wanna know the truth, I been all prayed out for about thirty years."

Then she flapped her hand in front of her face. "I like a cup of coffee at about this time," she said.

Rick Overlooking Horse didn't hug his grandmother, but he did put his hand on her arm. Mina looked at his hand for a moment. "For the love of mercy, the kettle got burned a hole in it. So now I ain't got no kettle." She closed her eyes and rocked back and forth on the backseat of the 1935 Ford coupe. "Oh, I've had the living dog kicked outta me."

Rick Overlooking Horse filled a pot from the 30-gallon plastic drum by the door and put it on the stove. He stoked the fire, added a log, and stoked it some more. Then he sat on the old wooden chair pulled up by the window. Through the greasy glass he could see the flung debris of a people born with the urge to move, but with nowhere to go; lawn chairs, old cars, buckets, a blanket, several sprung mattresses, a rusted-out oven.

"I heard that little Tapeworm went up north," Mina Overlooking Horse said. "But I 'spect he'll be back one of these days. He won't like all them fish them Indians eat." She wheezed some more. "Oh, my heart got badly broke and broke and broke. You don't know how badly broke." She grabbed at the flesh above her heart and gave it a squeeze.

The water started to boil. Rick Overlooking Horse got up and scooped some coffee into a cone of newspaper. The newsprint that came through the hot water gave the coffee an extra bitter taste, which Mina Overlooking Horse preferred to coffee without the taste of newsprint in it.

"I tell you something else." Mina took a sip of her coffee and sighed. "Three whole bags of sugar that little Tapeworm ate to get himself outta the war you got yourself into. He better not come back here expecting me to wait on him hand and toe."

Thaté, Yet Again

Rick Overlooking Horse found a teepee some California hippies had discarded after their Rez dreams had frozen stiff half a winter into their experiment. Then he swapped almost everything he owned for a blanket, five pounds of cornmeal, a pound of buffalo jerky, a sack of beans, seeds, and a bucket of lard. After that, he moved out to a piece of empty land the other side of Porcupine Butte, southwest of Kyle village.

Some of Rick Overlooking Horse's Immediate Relations trekked out to see him in his meadow and grumbled that he should not move so far out into the middle of nowhere at a time like this. He was young. He was wounded. And his grandmother was old. She was seizing up. "You should stay and take care of her. Maybe she'll get her second wind."

But as far as Rick Overlooking Horse was concerned, he

and his grandmother were on a parallel journey. Wind was wind whether it was first wind, or second wind, or the breath of the Great Mystery.

Mina Overlooking Horse said to Rick Overlooking Horse, "What's all this talk around the place of you keeping me company? You never talk. You ain't no better company than a rock." It wasn't disrespectful of rocks the way she said it. She was just stating a fact.

Mina made a motion like she was trying to clear hair from her eyes. "No, no, no, we're done, you and me. You go ahead and do whatever it is you were put on this Earth here for. Whatever I was put here for, I've been and I've done it. And I ain't doing it again, no more."

Mina Overlooking Horse
Crosses (the Hell) Over

In spite of everything that had happened to her people and to her, Mina Overlooking Horse could never completely shake the feeling that she counted for something. No matter how many indignities and insults stacked up to prove her wrong, Mina could never quite get rid of the idea that her little haphazard piece of life was of consequence to someone, even if that someone was only herself.

Or maybe, even, Wakan Tanka.

Oh, Wakan Tanka.

This had better be a plan to reduce us to mettle.

Mina Overlooking Horse sat down on the back seat of the 1935 Ford coupe in a state of slightly stoned distraction, which is what comes of taking a large dose of sacred weed with strong coffee first thing in the morning, before eating.

Find the light, see the light, be the light through all this shit.

"Holy shit," Mina Overlooking Horse said suddenly, sitting bolt upright. "Oh, holy, holy, holy shit."

MINA OVERLOOKING
HORSE, 1904–1966

One of the Immediate Relations considered herself a medical expert on account of having spent a month in hospital in Scottsbluff after a series of suicide attempts culminating in an ultimately near-fatal mix of rainbow-colored prescription pills and purple over-the-counter cough medicine plus about five cans of urine-colored King Cobra.

I say *about* five cans, because there were originally fourteen, but not all of them stayed in the Suicidal Immediate Relation's stomach, not by a long shot.

The Suicidal Immediate Relation said it was obvious Mina had died of a massive stroke, and at peace. And All the Other Immediate Relations had to agree Mina looked much happier dead than she had ever looked alive. It was as if she had finally seen the answer to all of life's mysteries, and it was one vast cosmic joke.

She was also stark naked, which came as a bit of a shock, and was not as easy to rectify as you might hope. A few of the Immediate Relations tried to cover Mina up, but blankets slid off unless they were put all the way over her head. Then the spectacle was more obscene than ever: Mina's bare legs poking out from under a blanket. In the end, it took several of the Immediate Relations a full hour and a half to wrestle Mina into a respectable winter dress and lay her down on her bed. By which time they were all sweating.

"Already," said one of the Immediate Relations, wrinkling her nose. "She's turning. We should . . ."

"We should watch over our Little Mother Mina Overlooking Horse for a day and a half in the hope that she may revive," one of the Elder Relations interrupted.

"A day and a half! In this heat? That's gonna be . . ." But that Indian was silenced with a look that could have altered the orbit of heavenly bodies.

The Bright, Shining
Beginning of the End

Mina Overlooking Horse was sixty-two, which you couldn't really say was young or old, since so much of her life had been incidental and unaccounted for. It would be more true to say she was timeless, having been born in the No Time of her people, twenty years before Indians were officially made citizens of these United States, fifteen years after the Sioux were taken off their land, and a year after American Indians were technically guaranteed the vote.

In as much as that means anything.

They buried her at Wounded Knee in the family plot, near where her great uncle, Spotted Elk, had been felled by the 7th Cavalry on December 29, 1890. Spotted Elk, his head wrapped in a scarf, his arms like broken wings cocked at his sides, frozen in death, as if attempting to rise from the earth, not quite ready to be swallowed by it. They had stacked his body along with the other frozen bodies of the Lakota warriors, women, and children, and threw all three hundred of them into a mass grave.

Some say more, some say less.

So let's say, between one hundred and fifty, and three hundred Oglala Lakota.

Roughly.

Meantime, precisely twenty Congressional Medals of Honor for Valor were awarded to members of the 7th Cavalry for the so-called Battle of Wounded Knee, more than for any other military engagement in the history of the United States.

Perhaps not understanding the situation properly, and having made some other miscalculations, the White Man considered the Massacre at Wounded Knee to be the end of the Indian Wars.

So yes.

They put Mina Overlooking Horse in a hole next to that mass grave up there at Wounded Knee. And when the dust from their shovels kicked up and blew in their faces they thought of the bones and blood of their foremothers and forefathers, and they thought of the dust of those long-ago children who didn't get a chance to be any kind of age. They wept then for Mina, and for their people, and for the people that were to come. Oh, my Ancestors, those Indians wept.

They wept and wept until the Suicidal Immediate Relation sliced off the tip of her pinkie finger with a penknife. A person can't just start hacking off bits of her own flesh. I mean, yes and no. But mostly, no.

"Ow!" the Immediate Relation shouted. Then she started hopping about with her hand between her legs. "Shit," she said. "Shit. Shit, that really hurts."

After that, the funeral was pretty well over.

Tales of Longing, Belonging, and Camouflage Tricks That Didn't Work

Five years into her time at the Indian boarding school in Kansas, Mina Overlooking Horse had written to her mother.

> *"The clerk at the train station there says if I am to come home, it is ten dollars. I can leave without my trunk. None of them old clothes fit me anymore in any event. I can't stay. Yours truly."*

She had not signed a name, because the new English name she had been given did not belong to her, and she could not now imagine the soft sound, let alone the spelling, of her Lakota name, although it wasn't so hard.

Mina. Meaning, Eldest Daughter.

Her family did not have ten dollars to send. So Mina walked back to the Rez. She was fifteen years old, and the walk took her three months. Her body grew lean and sinewy. She learned to move like a coyote, trotting in the shadows by day, traveling cross-country at night, eating on the run from the roadside garbage bonanza. Her feet bled, then their soles cracked and hardened like horse leather. So too did her heart, mostly.

One day in late August, walking along an undefended stretch of road in Oklahoma, Mina suddenly saw that her suffering would not be over. This was it. She was walking it; the sun, the sterilized earth, the hostility. And after this walk, there would be another walk like it. Mina's life would not improve. The blow of this information staggered her.

She was ready to lie down, to let breath leave her body and not return.

She didn't. But it's a miracle that she didn't.

Or as they say on the Rez, "Somehow."

Somehow she didn't.

Somehow she didn't lie down and die right there and then.

When she was sixteen, Thompson White Feather, a man of moderate temper and immoderate drinking habits, took Mina under his roof and in return she submitted uncomplainingly to his apologetic and infrequent advances. Before he died from a calcified liver at the age of thirty-five, Mina Overlooking Horse bore Thompson White Feather three children, all boys. And in due time, when the Bureau of Indian Affairs came to register her sons, she wrote their names thus:

Nobody Overlooking Horse.
Anybody Overlooking Horse.
Somebody Overlooking Horse.

She figured there was no power in those names, and in this way she hoped misfortune might overlook her children. But Nobody died of pneumonia his first winter away in boarding school, with nothing to stop the sickening ghosts from blowing right through him in that distant, flat place. And Anybody died on the Rez of diseases contracted during his stint as an airman in New Guinea, surviving malaria and typhus, surviving long enough to father Rick Overlooking Horse, but not surviving subsequent fevers long enough to see him born. Only Somebody stayed in the land of the living.

"Although God knows how," Mina said.

From an early age, Somebody Overlooking Horse behaved like a person with a dozen lives to spare: He fell out of trees, hit his head on the bottom of rivers, swallowed gasoline and burped fumes for a week. He survived a terrible stint in France as a soldier in the U.S. Army, he slept though a flood in Arkansas, he was knocked unconscious in an earthquake in California and awoke to find himself on the local news.

He escaped a house fire in Minnesota, he walked unscathed from four separate car crashes in four separate states, and he accidentally won a drunken gunfight in a bar in Gordon, Nebraska.

After all that, perhaps figuring nothing could kill him, Somebody took up bronco riding. Subsequently he courted death every Friday, Saturday, and most Wednesday nights at rodeos from California to Oklahoma. Like all those other men beating themselves senseless against the flanks of a flying bull, or a cat-shaped horse, Somebody was looking in vain for an external pain that would come close to matching the other, nameless internal pain.

So far, broken ribs, smashed molars, a pulverized ear, a broken nose, a broken jaw, and crushed testicles manifested to Somebody as little more than a dull annoyance, a slight hindrance. When he was knocked completely unconscious for a week, came out of it, rode six seconds on a saddle bronc in Reno before smacking himself out again on the arena fence, Mina said: "It's hard to tell why he doesn't just shoot hisself and be done with it."

How to Make a(n Honest)
Living on the Rez

A man has to eat, but out of pity for a people who seemed just as hurt by their prosperity as they were by their poverty, and out of concern for his own spiritual hygiene, Rick Overlooking Horse decided never to lay so much as the tip of a single finger on the diseased currency of the White Man, not even in the form of his military pension or his disability allowance. Many of his Immediate Relations were incensed. "Ayeee," one of them said. "Complete loss of the eye, code 6063. Do you know what that's worth?"

Another said, "It's the only way we're worth anything to them. Give 'em an eye. Give 'em an arm. Give 'em a leg. Heck, give 'em an eye, an arm, *and* a leg. A whole, healthy, working Indian ain't worth the skin he's in to the U.S. government."

Rick Overlooking Horse rigged up a greenhouse of windowpanes salvaged from an abandoned White Man's farm on the Rez border and grew a crop of potatoes, beans, squash, and spinach. Then he dug up a section of the meadow that got the best of the morning sun, and he planted a crop of corn, a row of potatoes, and a patch of Wahupta.

In four months he had his first half-pound harvest of the sacred weed. It was the perfect way for him to make a living. For a start, what's to say? He handed people twisted buds from the healing plant and they handed him a bushel of corn, or a sack of salt, or a bag of coffee, or maybe they sang him a song or two, and no money need change hands.

So in spite of what some of his Immediate Relations had predicted, Rick Overlooking Horse was never lonely on his land out there beyond Porcupine Butte. Not only were there enough men and women in need of herbal medicine to keep him abreast of the latest Rez gossip, but also the meadow around his teepee started to fill bit by bit with creatures that must have felt comforted by his presence. First ravens, rabbits, field mice, then a family of coyotes and an owl, and finally one summer morning an old buffalo bull wandered into view, as if he'd finally found the place he wished to retire.

The old bull had a brand on his rump, but Rick Overlooking Horse didn't put much credibility in human ownership of the sacred Tatanka, so he never bothered to find out from whose sacrilegious ranch the old bull had escaped. On cold nights the bull lay up against the teepee and Rick Overlooking Horse found he was comforted by the sound of the great creature chewing his cud, the rumble of his breathing.

On hot days, the two of them lazed in the shade of the cottonwood trees, where a little ground spring coursed west. Rick Overlooking Horse dangled his feet in the little stream and watched dragonflies. The old bull scratched himself against the trees' rough bark and cropped the sweet bluegrass that grew along the bank.

Summer moved through the meadow as waves of color.

The tender purples and yellows first.

Locoweed, flax, bluebells, mustard.

Then a wave of white and pink.

Geraniums, chickweed, yarrow, and roses.

And then, just before the hottest week of the summer, a riot of blooms, balms, and cures of all colors.

Beard tongue, prickly pear, field mint, catnip, mullein, aster.

The whisper of dandelion gone to seed.

Rick Overlooking Horse Accidentally Becomes a Medicine Man, a Chief, an Elder

Things got around, as things do on the Rez, that Rick Overlooking Horse was war-returned, and whatever he'd seen and done over there, it had fixed him up in an uncommon way, so now he was also a man of rare wisdom. And after that, people started to go to him with their wounded hearts and curdled souls. Drug addicts and alcoholics, newlyweds and spurned lovers, soldiers going to war and soldiers coming back.

The Lakota Oglala don't have words like chief, and elder, and medicine man the way the White Man does. And still the White Man can't help himself, "Take me to your leader."

Perhaps it is beyond the imagination of the White Man that some people live together not in hierarchy but in stages, and circles, and cycles.

Rick Overlooking Horse simply became. Everyone knows there is nothing more powerful or difficult. And that it is often necessary to have a guide out of all the noisy unbecoming we do between birth and death.

Rick Overlooking Horse, thinking of nothing better, sent them with some Wahupta and water for as many days as they needed into the middle of the meadow. Sit on an empty stomach and an open mind in the full force of the weather and stare at nothing but prairie grass and an old bull buffalo long enough, and eventually you might see yourself in the old buffalo bull.

Or in a blade of grass that feeds the old bull buffalo.

Or in the thin skid of a cloud in the sky that will soon water the blade of grass that feeds the old buffalo bull.

Buffalo, or Tatanka.

Tatanka. Meaning, He Who Owns Us.

Everyone is born knowing this: We cannot be unless we first belong. Soil is flesh in waiting; flesh is soil in waiting. We spend years forgetting this, and the return to that knowledge is always painful, never easy.

Meditation, vision quest, hamblechya, childbirth, grief, prayer, proper and rigorous intoxication; they say there are many ways to the summit of the mountain. The people who exhaust themselves are the ones who run around the base of the mountain shrieking that theirs is the only real, proper way to the top.

Although Rick Overlooking Horse didn't see the point of saying any of this.

Time will teach, he figured.

World will teach.

The Old Buffalo Bull,
Again

Seasons turned. Rain turned into mist, and mist turned into clouds of steel grey. The Thunder Beings shook the earth, tossed the cottonwood trees, and threw bolts of lightning to the ground. Then after two or three moons, temperatures plummeted, the little stream froze, the cottonwood trees let their leaves fall, and the clouds drifted landward in thin sheets and then piles of snow. A few moons after that, the snow receded and the little stream began to run again, and the leaves of the cottonwoods emerged, lime green and shiny.

Then the cycle started over again.

The third winter of their time together, the old buffalo grew gaunt. Rick Overlooking Horse procured a few bales of alfalfa but the old bull turned his head from the offer of the food that smelled too much like his long years of captivity, and Rick Overlooking Horse felt chastened by the implicit reprimand. After that, he let the creature find his own way home.

The old bull lay in the meadow day after night after day with his back to the wind, his coat clotted with snow so that he looked more like a drift than anything alive. Finally, on the afternoon of the shortest day of that third winter, the great creature's spirit surrendered.

Rick Overlooking Horse wafted sage over the old bull's body, skinned the beast, sprinkled the hide with salt and stretched it out on lodgepole saplings. Thereafter, he kept watch as the family of coyotes sang and yipped around the carcass of the old bull, and the ravens gurgled and tut-tutted, and a pair of bald eagles sawed south from the Bad River on the scent of carrion.

The following thaw, Rick Overlooking Horse awoke one morning to find another old buffalo bull had wandered into the meadow. There was no brand on this bull's hide. "Hau kola," Rick Overlooking Horse said. The buffalo lay next to the teepee at nights, and on hot summer days he scratched himself against the cottonwood trees by the creek and cropped the sweet grass. He allowed ravens and magpies to settle on his coat and to comb for parasites.

And so it went.

Seasons turned, and turned again.

Rick Overlooking Horse
and the Ugly Red Stud

Once a year, so that he did not lose the habits of his fellow humans completely, Rick Overlooking Horse walked twenty miles cross-country into the town of Pine Ridge for the annual Lakota Indian Rodeo. It was at this rodeo on a hot Saturday afternoon in the already baking August of 1969 that Rick Overlooking Horse came into possession of the hardiest, and possibly the wisest, stud to commit seed to the brood mares of Turtle Island in seven generations.

In those days the Lakota Indian Rodeo was an even wilder affair than it is now. Cowboys and Indians came from Wyoming, Nebraska, South Dakota, Arizona, Montana, Utah, and from Indian reservations across the West. Decent bucking stock was brought in from a contractor in Garfield County. Entry fees were steep, twenty dollars a shot, back then when a loaf of bread cost twenty-three cents, and it was winner take all. Bookies set up stands and trade was brisk. Mexicans from Nogales set up kiosks and sold enchiladas and tamales. Indians set up shelters under old tarpaulins and sold fry bread and stew.

The undisputed champion bareback rider in a three-state area at that time was Rick Overlooking Horse's uncle, Somebody. Although, at first glance, the horse Somebody drew wasn't anything to put your money on. It was mostly blotchy red with white freckles on its haunches, a pink face, and four white hooves. It had a prominent nose and pale eyes that suggested cunning rather than intelligence. Its hind end looked chewed up and it sloped at the shoulder, like it had started life as something else, wilder than a horse, and changed its mind at the last minute.

"Well that's a nonstarter," one of the Immediate Relations said. "You'd be better off riding a freaking wheelbarrow."

But when Somebody lowered himself on the Ugly Red Stud's back, the muscles from the animal's chest to its haunches contracted, and its neck swelled. "Yep," Somebody said. "It goes." He gripped the rigging. The horse battled the gates, stomping and kicking. Cowboys had to scramble out of the way. Somebody smiled. "Let's dance," he said.

The chute was opened; Somebody brushed his spurs lightly up the Ugly Red Stud's shoulders. The horse gathered itself from its haunches, and released up and up, twisting into the air a whole twelve feet before flipping nearly backward on a hot-touch landing. Somebody Overlooking Horse paddled the air with his toes, his left hand whipping above his head. The Ugly Red Stud pirouetted skyward again, and again. Somebody pressed all his weight into his ankles, turned his face to the sky, and laughed. Those close to him say they saw tears on his cheeks.

Eight seconds of pure beauty. Even the Mexicans from Nogales who'd seen everything in Tijuana and Sonora agreed there'd never been a ride like it in their lifetimes; such an unexpected partnership. As if Somebody had finally met his soul's partner in this strange, ugly, untried creature. The eight-second bell rang. The crowd cheered. A Lot of Relations started streaming to the bookies to collect their winnings.

But the Ugly Red Stud and Somebody were still bucking around the arena. Then, seeing the pickup men come for him, the Ugly Red Stud stopped bucking, flattened himself, and bulleted out of the arena—which is to say, out of the circle of pickups and station wagons, and lawn chairs—in such a blur it took a while for the crowd to start laughing, and then gasping, at the sight of Somebody and the Ugly Red Stud making dust far out onto the prairie.

The pickup men, experienced Indians all, plus one good Cowboy from Cheyenne, used up three sets of horses going out for them. Time after time after time they came back for fresh mounts, shaking their heads and sweating rivers. That Ugly Red Stud was still making for the Black Hills, they said, with Somebody riding along with a smile on his face like he'd been kissed by God.

They said it looked like he'd stopped caring if he'd been at it eight seconds, eight hours, or half the week. They said he looked delirious with joy. So they gave up sending good horses after bad and came back without either man or beast.

The rest of the rodeo went on. First the rest of bucking horses, then the calf roping, and then the bull riding. After that people began packing up their lawn chairs and quilts and picnics and going home. Even the concessionaire from Garfield, Nebraska, who had brought the bucking stock in the first place, was all loaded up, except for the Ugly Red Stud. He waited, and looked at his watch and waited some more. Finally, he spat and looked at the sky.

"Tell you what," he said to Rick Overlooking Horse, the only Indian left at the rodeo grounds. "Give me fifty bucks and if that horse ever comes back, he's yours. And I don't care what you do with him. You can break him, you can shoot him, or you can eat him. He's an Injun horse anyway, roped him myself off a band south of here a couple seasons back."

Rick Overlooking Horse considered the man's offer for a few silent minutes.

"Okay, thirty," the Cowboy conceded, spitting again. "Or what you got. I'll take what you got." He eyed the sky irritably. "This weather ain't waiting for no one."

Rick Overlooking Horse removed a small bag of Wahupta

from his shirt pocket and showed it to the Cowboy. The Cowboy looked over his shoulder, and then he dipped his nose in the bag. "Okay," he said stuffing the bag into his jacket and hauling himself into his rig. "You got yourself a deal. And you have yourself a grand old Injun war reenactment of a time, you ever catch the son of a bitch."

The Cowboy laughed so hard he had to thump on his chest to restart his lungs. Rick Overlooking Horse chuckled too. That should have said something to the Cowboy, but by then his rig was all revved up, his beams were on bright, and he was burning rubber all the way home.

Indian War Ponies

Rick Overlooking Horse never did ride the Ugly Red Stud, didn't even try, but in time he swapped several pounds of Wahupta for a few brood mares, hardy Indian ponies with good bones, independent minds, and vivid coloring. The subsequent colts were born able to make a living on marginal Rez soils; they showed up knowing all about wind and ice; they had unbeatable legs and unbreakable lungs. They'd ride into a hail of bullets, take flight off cliffs, or plunge into rapids for the right rider.

It's hard to explain how two nations so freshly acquainted—the Oglala Lakota Oyate and the horse—could have been such fast, easy, elegant companions. But it was as if tributary met tributary, blood flowed into blood. The Lakota and the horse met as sisters and brothers and together they were something more than either nation could produce on its own.

So it was with Rick Overlooking Horse and the Ugly Red Stud. They saw each other, and an ancient contract was fulfilled. It was as if they were each able to see, in each other's strengths and disfigurements, a fellow sufferer. By which I mean that since suffering is the only way to wisdom, they saw in one another a fellow soul of great sagacity. And they found in each other's minds a place of tranquil solace.

Pony Trading

Cowboys from Wyoming with a thing about conquering the wind, polo players from California with a thing about speed, Scandinavians with a thing about Indians—they all found Rick Overlooking Horse's herd the best place to acquire a mount of such stubborn stamina; it was well known that the only way to slow one down, let alone stop one, was to put a bullet between its ears while you were still up there on the saddle. They were that good.

And the crazy, one-eyed, silent Indian would give them away.

Literally give them away.

For strips of cured leather, or fishing poles, or for nothing, you could get yourself a war pony with legs of steel and limitless lungs. Some of the Scandinavian women made it obvious they were prepared to pay for their horses in kind, as it were, a body for a body. A few begged to be allowed to stay in the teepee forever, with the one-eyed, quiet Indian, but although Rick Overlooking Horse seemed quite happy to accommodate them under the old buffalo bull's hide for a night or two, he had no intention of making a life of trouble for himself.

Trouble

Anyway, by the early 1970s on the Pine Ridge Indian Reservation, you didn't have to make trouble for yourself. Trouble saved you the effort, and came looking for you. Indians fed up with the way things were broken, angered with the way their people's souls had soured up from generations of abuse in those boarding schools, sick of seeing their reservations marinated in grief and trauma, joined up with other Indians.

The effort was to repair the Indian way of life, restore Indian spirituality and culture.

The intention was to hear the old ways again, to get clear of the scorching White wind that had come so devastatingly from the east, and from the south.

Across the Rez, warrior societies formed.

They called themselves the American Indian Movement.

AIM, for short.

There was anger and outrage and confusion. An Indian was shot in the back by her only son. It was all a terrible accident; he'd been firing over her head. But there he was with her blood on his hands, shouting loudly as if his angry denial could undo what had been done. That was the atmosphere all over the Rez those long, violent years in the late 1960s and early 1970s when anything felt possible, and everything seemed chaotic and urgent.

You Choose What Son
Comes Home

Initially, You Choose was not very successful breaking into the drug-dealing racket in New York State. He talked a big talk, but he was frightened of the city ghettos where his bosses said he should go, certain he'd be knifed by a Puerto Rican or brought to his knees by a sky-walking Mohawk. And he didn't like the poverty-struck rural routes either with the scary White people. They looked far too thin and jittery and mentally fragile to be the casual owners of so many guns.

So he played it safe and sold hard drugs to kids in the rotted-out school districts on the edge of old Indian territory. This made You Choose a fairly decent living, but it eventually made the People of the Great Hill angry with him, and then his bosses displayed a loss of humor.

"At least the kid wasn't an Indian," You Choose said. "Or

maybe he was just part Indian. And he wasn't so young. He had facial hair. Show me a Indian kid with facial hair," You Choose laughed.

Nobody else did.

You Choose threw up his hands. "Okay, okay. So you don't like me working here, I'm gone," he said. "Watch me go."

They watched him go.

That night in a bar in Niagara Falls, You Choose drank his eight whiskies straight with beer chasers.

"When they find out who I am, they gonna wish they treated me with more respect," he told a woman on a stool next to him. He was laboring under a heavy bloom of drunkenness.

"Yeah?" the woman said.

"Yeah, I'm You Shoes," You Choose said, his forefinger diving into the bar counter. "Watch Son."

"Oh yeah?" the woman said.

"I'm going home," You Choose said. "To the Rez. They're having a war."

"Huh."

"Yeah. Wanna come?"

The woman got up. "No," she said.

You Choose hiccupped, then swayed violently. "Is it 'cos I'm Indian?" he shouted at the woman's disappearing back.

High Noon on the North American Plains, and Why It Is Better to Meet Some Other Time

Rick Overlooking Horse did not seem surprised to see You Choose appear in a battered 1963 Ford Falcon station wagon, a dark grey ribbon of exhaust against a sun-bleached sky.

"Hau," You Choose said, leaning out the window with a cigarette between his teeth. He turned off the motor. "Long time no see, Ricky boy," You Choose said.

He got out of the car and stared at Rick Overlooking Horse's setup; the teepee, the greenhouse, the vegetable garden, the old bull buffalo and the Indian war ponies grazing in the meadow. "It looks like you got yourself a movie set, man." He laughed to show he was mocking his Rez cousin. Then he threw his cigarette onto the ground and crushed it out with the heel of his boot, and coughed. "They say Mina finally died," he said.

"Han," Rick Overlooking Horse said, nodding.

You Choose was moving around an awful lot for a man who wasn't making any distance at all over ground. He crossed his arms, shifted his heels about, and lit another cigarette. Then he made a gesture toward Rick Overlooking Horse. "Well, they sure messed you up nicely over there."

"Han," Rick Overlooking Horse agreed again.

After that, neither man said anything for a long time. The dog-day cicadas shrilled from the cottonwoods, ravens lazily trundled across the heavy sky, on the horizon storm clouds banked, a pair of fat robins plopped about on the damp grass, a rabble of pine white butterflies puddled in a shallow rain pool. You Choose fidgeted.

"They say you're a medicine man," You Choose said at last.

Rick Overlooking Horse shook his head.

"Are you?"

"No," Rick Overlooking Horse said.

There was another long silence.

"Or what are you then?"

Rick Overlooking Horse said, "I'm a janitor."

You Choose laughed, but his laugh caught as a cough. He smacked himself on the chest. "Huh, that's a good one man. Very far out."

Rick Overlooking Horse flinched.

"My brother," You Choose said. "I was thinking I could use, you know, some wisdom. Some directions from the fucking ancestors." You Choose coughed again. "Or, what have you. A vision, if you will."

Rick Overlooking Horse looked at the ground for a long time with distracted concentration, as if listening carefully for a very faint sound. Then he turned, ducked into his teepee, and reemerged with a bowl of water, a bag of Wahupta, a pipe, and a box of matches. He handed these to You Choose.

He didn't tell You Choose What Son to sit in the meadow until he could see himself in a blade of grass, or in the great Tatatanka, or in a wisp of wind. He didn't tell him to surrender.

Instead he said, "There is nowhere you can go to reach the Great Spirit or to leave the Great Spirit. Stay where you are."

The Transmission

You Choose What Son had not sat hamblechya since he and Rick Overlooking Horse were fifteen. That summer they were sent up to the bluffs on the edge of the Mako Sica by a grumpy elder with about a dozen other boys, all of them scattered about that place like discarded baggage.

That had been bad enough.

Why, You Choose What Son asked himself a couple of hours into his present vision quest, was he doing it again? He remembered from last time that it had been a terrible experience. Hot, of course, and thirsty but also lonely and baffling. And, honestly, he hadn't received any vision. Although he pretended he had. And he suspected everyone else of pretending too. The pretending became a little bit real after that.

And not everything was pretending. After all, You Choose reasoned, he may not have had a vision, but he'd cried for one, and suffered for it, and that was enough evidence for You Choose to wield his hamblechya around like a weapon.

And if you were Indian, it was what you did. The way the White Man—even the all-sinning, God-denying White Man—was forced to submit to God.

Now You Choose What Son's lips cracked. The sun sang in his ears. At night, the temperatures dropped like a stone, and he shivered and would have sobbed with self-pity if there had been anyone around to tend his tears. He wanted more than anything to leave this place, and stretch his limbs. He wanted food, fried preferably and with salt. But then he thought of how he'd be mocked in the village if he came back before his time, looking too pale and unmarked. What was needed, he felt, were blisters and sunburn. His eyes welled at the thought of the hero's welcome he'd get at Big Bat's when he came back all hamblechya-bruised. People would congratulate him, and respect him. They'd ask him if he received his vision.

You Choose sat and he sat. He nodded off a few times, jerked awake by the hard ground. Sometimes, he felt he was flying over the land, and others that he was being slowly baked into it. Then finally, two days later, in the hot early afternoon, the transmission from the Great Mystery came to You Choose What Son in *exactly* these words:

Peace, y'all.

By this somewhat surprising opening gambit, You Choose What Son knew it was the Great Mystery talking, and not his own imagination.

The Great Mystery wishes to let it be known that They are infinite and expansive.

Ha ha.
The laughter took You Choose aback.

The Great Mystery is all things and the Great Mystery is the center of all things.

In a terrible, sudden moment, You Choose saw everything that has happened and would ever happen in a great pulsing ball of energy. He saw the beginning of the world as we know it, and its end. And then he saw its beginning again. He saw these in slight interruptions of light in an otherwise somewhat steady pulse. He saw the entire duration of human existence as little more than a tiny pop of pale yellow somewhere on the edge of the ball.

You Choose said, "That's *all*?"

It was all.

And it was all too much.

But They would like it to be remembered—the Great Mystery continued—there is always only infinity.
Ha ha.

Written like this, it makes it sound as if the transmission from the Great Mystery happened swiftly, in fluid downloads. But it didn't. It came to You Choose What Son in threads, like smoke curling from a fire, gradually solidifying into words, then sentences, then a phrase. And then it settled into place, and You Choose knew that he'd heard all he could stand to hear.

That is all.
You know the rest.
Ha ha ha ha ha.
Ha ha ha ha ha ha.

The laughter was the worst thing of all. It was joyful. It rang. It pealed. It was everywhere. You Choose What Son gave a shriek and ran blindly from Rick Overlooking Horse's meadow covering his ears. He fled, wobbling, staggering, all the way down the muddy road from the teepee and into the blond, bleached, sandy lands along the edge of Rick Overlooking Horse's land.

Later that night, he drove the 1963 Ford Falcon to one of the liquor stores in Whiteclay and bought enough malt liquor to render him literally senseless for three whole days.

After that, he nursed a two-day hangover. And after that, he vowed never to seek a vision anywhere again.

Not everyone chooses to be liberated by liberating messages. Some people choose to be terrorized by them. And in this, you can only be what you are.

The Somewhat Accidental
Early Political Career of
You Choose What Son

All Indians know you can claim shelter with almost any other Indian on the face of Turtle Island almost any time you find yourself in need. But You Choose found he was short on Any Relation at All prepared to take him in.

They told him it was for his own health. "We have black mold," one of the More Immediate Relations said, coughing feebly.

You Choose didn't know how long he could sleep rough, but he did know wild horses could not drag him back to Rick Overlooking Horse's horrible hot meadow with that creepy bull buffalo, and that Ugly Red Stud.

He preferred being close to the big village, where the

half-breeds and the city-returned Indians lived. He hated the traditionalists and the full-bloods, with their braids and their Lakota language, and their warrior society tattoos. And above all, he hated Rick Overlooking Horse, out there in the middle of nowhere doing all his bogus medicine man, Big Chief Indian stuff.

When the weather turned, and it got too cold for him to sleep on the bottomed-out mattress behind the gas station, You Choose moved into a basement in a small, crowded house on the east edge of Pine Ridge with an ex-in-law of an aunt on his mother's side in exchange for thirty dollars a month in rent. There were twelve children and four adults in the small house, so You Choose spent much of the winter in the café at the gas station drinking weak coffee and complaining in a feeble, violent way about every injustice he could think of.

What happened next to You Choose proves the point, that a lot of what passes for success in a person's political career is actually just luck, or weather. Or, a bit of both. It was an unusually windy winter that year and while a body can dress against low temperatures, a howling wind is something against which there is little effective defense. People were driven indoors, into the café, where You Choose— mildly frenzied on a mix of resentment, insomnia, and low-grade caffeine—acquired an audience for his incessant stream of complaints.

His audience responded at first with nonchalance, and then with increasing interest. Because, when many of them came to think of it, they too shared You Choose's complaints. It was as if the Misery Olympics were underway in Pine Ridge that winter, and You Choose What Son was the anointed, undisputed champion of a large pack of also-rans.

The Campaign

By the beginning of spring, You Choose was so moved, humbled, and inspired by his own popularity, he decided to run for tribal chairman. He thought his odds of winning were excellent. He already had most of Pine Ridge village on his side; all he had to do was make inroads with the more traditional types in the outlying villages and meadows.

But then it got out, as things do on the Rez, that You Choose What Son's U.S. government-issued Certificate of Degree of Indian Blood said he was eight-sixteenths Lakota.

It didn't take a mathematician to divide that equation into a slur.

"That there's Mina Overlooking Horse's half-breed, ennit?" one of the older Indians said.

"Ayeee. His name were Watson, weren't it? Where did he go finding that What Son from?"

And they laughed, held their stomachs and roared. "Oh, ho-lay, yeah that's a good one! You Choose Your Own Name."

"Big warrior!"

But You Choose What Son wasn't in the mood to be mocked. He gave very long, angry speeches at the Pine Ridge Powwow Grounds about the missed economic opportunities on the Rez. Sometimes he said he supported his brothers and sisters out there campaigning for more Indian sovereignty. "Those Alcatraz Indians," he called them. Other times he seemed to be condemning the occupation of Alcatraz by American Indians.

Even a lightly dozing Indian spectator, just there for the possibility of a fry-up, could tell You Choose What Son's stories didn't line up, exactly. There were holes in his narrative, and much of what he said invited doubt and confusion. But that didn't jolt any of You Choose's supporters too badly. After all, it was 1972, and most of the human population of the world now had biographies with bits blown out of it, shredded, or missing. Most of the human population of the world seemed unable to say anymore what they believed, or who they were, or why they were here.

On Election Day, You Choose got into office by a margin of a hundred and twenty votes. The old-school Indians, the full-breeds, and the Elders were shocked. They had assumed the half-breed was unelectable. They had not noticed how he was appealing to the half-breeds, near-breeds, and wanna-breeds in and around the town of Pine Ridge. They had not seen how a fearful, frustrated person could make himself a leader of other fearful, frustrated people.

"Oh, but now he won't be good," they said. "First thing he'll do is order his face carved on the moon."

Nepotism, Just Between
Friends and Family

You Choose What Son exceeded even the Wise Elders expectations for bad governance. He appropriated tribal funds to buy himself an F-150 hot off the lot in Rapid City, all the trimmings. He appropriated even more tribal funds to build himself a proper sheetrock and siding house in Pine Ridge, with indoor plumbing, forced air, and working lights. He gave tribal support to those who turned a blind eye to his graft, and he withdrew tribal support from anyone who opposed him.

Threats began to plop onto You Choose What Son's doorstep. Complaints began to rain into the regional office of the Bureau of Indian Affairs. You Choose formed a private militia—Guardians of the Oglala Nation, or GOONs to intimidate anyone who seemed likely to expose him. He fired a handful of people on no grounds other than he felt like it. He hired friends. "There's nothing in tribal law against nepotism," he was quoted as saying in the *Lakota Country Times*.

In order to avoid restlessness when roads remained in states of disrepair, when schools closed because of striking teachers, and when water ran out in all the villages, You Choose held exciting political events at the Pine Ridge Powwow Grounds. He encouraged his supporters to practice their war cries. He roared when they shot a few rounds in the air. "In-dee-in! In-dee-in!" he chanted, rather pointlessly, but to great effect.

Merchants in Whiteclay did a brisk trade in guns, knives, malt liquor, and whisky. Full-bloods battled half-bloods openly in the streets of Pine Ridge town. FBIs, they called themselves. Full-blood Indians. Urban-returned Indians, confused by their years in cities across the nation, clashed with each other over which among them had been the most colonized by the White Man's ways. Colonized Indian Asses, they called each other. CIA, for short. A lot of Indians were very drunk much of the time. Everyone was perplexed.

As soon as night fell there was the chattering and popping of gunfire in all the villages, and the murder rate on the Rez exceeded that of Detroit, New York, and Los Angeles. In homes across the Rez, people switched out the lights, blew out candles, and put boards and blankets over their windows as soon as it was dark. Brothers split between sides, one staying out in the windswept south, and the other heading into the village of Pine Ridge. It felt like a mass-murder–suicide pact, which is, if you think about it, the ultimate fulfillment of an attempted genocide.

A Warning

T hink about it.

If the people of a nation are violently forced to forget themselves, their sacred traditions, their ways of life, their understanding of the Earth, their respect for other nations, then what follows is almost inevitable: The men will take out their amnesia on the women, the women will take it out on the children, and everyone will take it out on the land.

This goes for all nations, of course, not just the White Man Nation.

But some of the Original People believe that if they follow the ways of the White Man Nation, it will save them from this death. They believe it will save their children from death if they slip into White, but of course any time we become something other than ourselves, it is just death by another name.

Why does the White Man have such a terror of love?

The things that will eventually happen to all of us have to happen to the White Man first, because everything must go around and around. There is no other way, obviously. In all their fear and killing, they don't know that it is for their sakes too that we so stubbornly refuse to forget ourselves in all our love and nature. So that when at last exhausted, bloodied, raped and raping they reach us, they'll find us here.

Right where they left us.

Think about it.

Meantime, on the Moon

On December 11, 1972, the spaceship Apollo 17 landed on the moon. It was the last time humans left Earth's low orbit. Which is to say, it was the last time humans sped past 1,243 miles above sea level, through medium Earth orbit and into the vast, tranquil-seeming space known as high Earth orbit, beyond which we know only what scientists and sages can tell us, inferred back to us from their imaginations, calculations, and probing missions.

Still, no one on Earth knows the answer to the ultimate question: "But then what?"

Eugene "Gene" Cernan stepped onto the lunar surface in the Taurus-Littrow lunar valley, and was hit by the full force of the sun. He said, "Oh, my golly. Unbelievable. Unbelievable. But is it bright in the sun." He sounded both ecstatic and blinded. But also as if his voice had been put in a tin and left without air for a long time.

As Eugene "Gene" Cernan was leaving the moon, he said, "We leave as we came," which seemed an odd thing to say. Like saying, "Our having been here is the same as our not having been here." Or, "We want nothing more from this experience than this experience." But, if you kept listening, he kept talking. In fact, there were whole other clauses to his sentence. "And, God willing, as we shall return, with peace and hope for all mankind."

Perhaps it was too much to say.

And maybe he didn't say it well.

He didn't sound pensive, as he might have were he in a movie of his life, instead of in his actual life. He didn't sound wistful, like it was the beginning of every wonderful thing. Like we'd see ourselves the way he did—mere ideas of energy on a breathtakingly beautiful and utterly improbable planet—and would therefore fall too in love with ourselves to keep up the killing.

Like now we'd seen, and now we couldn't unsee the truth.

Like we'd change our ways, and do better.

Instead, Eugene "Gene" Cernan sounded trounced, as if now he'd actually, really seen, and now couldn't unsee the truth. It was as if he knew there and then that it was going to take something more than human intelligence to get us out of the trouble we were in. We would never change our ways. We couldn't figure out on our own what better was.

Did the White Man Take Smallpox to the Moon, and Other Good Obvious Questions

There were some Indians on the Rez who paid attention to the fact that there was a mission to the moon, and that among the astronauts was a White Man expressing hope and peace for all mankind.

But what were you supposed to make of a White Man on the moon when there had been violence and nothing but violence on Indian land for so long? And now the place was burning up, it was on fire. You'd hear something like that, from a White Man like Eugene "Gene" Cernan on the moon of all places, you'd shake your head and get on with the war at hand.

Those poor aliens don't have a clue what's about to happen to them.

"Burn the blankets they give you!"

Someone shot fourteen rounds from a 1951 AK-47 assault rifle into the air and howled a great, terrible, heartfelt war cry.

And so it went on, through the fall and into winter, and past the longest darkness of the season, when the constellation of stars known as the Racetrack was at its zenith, on and on, into the deep cold nights of the Moon of Hard Times.

Oh, All My Lakota Relations, that winter was wicked for its violence.

The Second Siege of
Wounded Knee

On the morning of February 20, 1973, Rick Overlooking Horse collected up the old buffalo hide, a small, black, three-legged pot, a sack of beans, a pound of buffalo jerky, and a bag of cornmeal. He roped a filly out of the Ugly Red Stud's herd, put a headstall on her, threw his provisions across her withers, and then vaulted onto her back. Then he rode past the bluffs, past Porcupine Butte toward Wounded Knee hill until the sun was low in the western sky.

When he came to the creek, he crossed it, cut above the willows and through the snow-crusted sagebrush meadow, on toward the cemetery and the little white church. Once he reached the top of the hill, he dismounted and set the filly loose to forage on whatever she could find. With the last of the day's thin light, he made a snow wall against the wind. After that, he coaxed a low fire into life. He melted snow in the pot. Before the cold had time to settle in his bones, Rick Overlooking Horse ate a little cornmeal and salt. Then he wrapped himself in the old buffalo bull's hide and slept.

By the end of a week, other Indians from around Pine Ridge and other reservations around the country had joined Rick Overlooking Horse. They silently drifted into the small, makeshift camp in groups of three or four, then dozens, and scores, and finally hundreds.

The Indians vowed to stage a peaceful standoff at Wounded Knee until further notice. They made three demands: The removal of the tribal chairman; the restoration of treaty negotiations with the U.S. government; and the return of Hé Sapa to the Oceti Sakowin Oyate, to the People of the Seven Council Fires.

Hé Sapa

According to the Oglala Lakota Oyate, and the standard theories of cosmology, there is no center to the universe. It is everywhere. So the Lakota are not wrong to say, "This here, where we are, is the center of our sacred lands." Here, right here, where since 1941 there have been the outsized faces of four American presidents carved into the granite batholith.

Hé Sapa. Meaning, Black Hills.

The Length of a Siege

A siege makes a single day appear to last longer than the time it takes for the sun to break over the prairie hills, span the sky, then vanish behind the pine bluffs. When you're doing it, a siege is more than a full-time job. It's a full-time life.

Quite aside from the issue at hand, people cannot divorce themselves from hunger, or from the need to relieve their bowels, or from exhaustion. There is nothing romantic about being cold, weary, and frightened. It's easy to forget this about social movements. People don't cause chaos, foment rebellion, and use their own bodies as a form of stubborn protest because they have nothing else to do. People do these things because they have nothing else to lose.

Find wood, cut wood, tend fire. Melt snow, make food. Mud takes over and is in everything. It's in the skin of the people, and in their clothing. It's in the pressing, public ache of bowels shot through with fire.

Oh, All My Ancestors.

How much strength must one people have?

And for how long must they have it?

It's excessively wearying, All My Relations, excessively wearying.

The End of the Siege

The siege went on and on and on.

Days rolled into weeks.

Each day grew a little longer, by which I mean, not only did the days feel as if they started sooner and ended later— the makeshift latrines more overflowing, the food thinner— but also they were literally longer. The sun lingered in the sky for a moment more each day. The redwing blackbirds began massing in the willows along the creek. The snow began to recede up the south slopes of the cemetery and the smell of tree sap ran sharp in the air.

A journalist in Rapid City got wind of the siege and the local media descended. Rick Overlooking Horse broke his customary silence. "Tribal violence is a corruption to the Oglala Lakota Oyate, and what is a corruption around one of our Seven Fires becomes a corruption to all." Although it was mostly the photograph of his war-melted face that made the headline stand out: "WOUNDED VIETNAM VETERAN SPEAKS OUT FOR INDIAN RIGHTS."

A few dozen United States Marshals were sent in to the Rez.

In the United States, domestic war looks a lot like a foreign invasion.

It doesn't hurt that the enemies of the federation are almost always Black or Brown, except for the occasional nonbreeding pairs of pro-peace homosexual Communists or anorexic vegan lesbians. Or those South American–influenced Jesuits, with their freakishly calm attitude toward physical violence, although they're also typically nonbreeding, and most popes can be counted on to frown upon them.

You Choose What Son strutted behind the marshals with a bullhorn, going on and on about rule of law until someone on the Indian side popped a bullet in his direction. Then he screamed, dropped his bullhorn, and ducked for cover. Which was just as well for him. In the next hours, days, and weeks, half a million rounds of ammunition were exchanged.

"Those AIM terrorists are the only major Indian problem," You Choose said. "They're just bums trying to get their braids and mugs in the press."

On the sixty-ninth day of the siege, Rick Overlooking Horse sat with the other Elders. After two days of silent contemplation, prayer, and discussion, they decided a truce should be called. And on the morning of the seventy-first day of the siege, Rick Overlooking Horse scattered the last of his tobacco for the crossing-over spirits. Then he stood up, and he walked toward the guns of the U.S. Marshals like he didn't care if he lived or died. The filly trotted after him, enjoying moving over decent ground again after such a long time on the frozen mud.

Rick Overlooking Horse roped her then, and when she'd stopped fighting his capture, he offered the filly to a U.S. Marshal. "Take her," he said.

No one moved.

Rick Overlooking Horse said, "Wacantognaka."

He flicked the end of the rope at the U.S. Marshal.

The marshal swallowed. "Stand down, man!"

Rick Overlooking Horse dropped the rope, turned his back on the U.S. Marshal, and walked away, knowing that for as far as a crow could fly there was a rifle trained between the blades of his shoulders.

He noticed the ground was soft now, vigorous shoots of grass pushing up here and there where mud had forced an early melt.

He heard a redwing blackbird trill from the willows.

The air was raw with the smell of melting manure.

In late May agents from the U.S. Department of Justice arrested the leaders of the Siege of Wounded Knee and charged them with incitement to riot. A month later, a judge in Minnesota dismissed the case.

By the time Rick Overlooking Horse returned to the meadow, it was mid-June.

All the mares had foaled, and he was a full crop rotation behind in the garden.

For a nation with such a professed obsession about the cost and price of time, the White Man is very careless with the other people's seasons.

Meantime, Mean Time

You Choose What Son knew that Rick Overlooking Horse and the other leaders of the Wounded Knee Siege would go down in history as heroes, and that he would be dismissed as a half-breed sellout and that knowledge gnawed at his soul like a junkyard rat. Sometimes, he wished he'd stood up to that Indian bullet instead of ducking.

Provided the bullet had only nicked him, of course.

You Choose riled up his GOONs. He reminded them of all the insults—real and imagined—that might have been aimed in their direction. He provided them with malt liquor for their veins and gasoline for their cars. Then he made sure to have a front seat to enjoy the conflagration.

People took to boarding up their windows night and day to stop stray bullets, preferring to live in perpetual darkness rather than to risk flying glass. Schools across the Rez closed, and children were sent home. The only gas station on the Rez was set on fire, and the blaze roared for days. It seemed as if You Choose What Son was determined to get his revenge on every man, woman, and child on the Rez.

You Choose What Son's Fit of Rage

You Choose What Son's clay-splattered pickup roared into the meadow, careening over the season's first snow and sending the ravens and magpies tumbling skyward.

"I'm going to get you, you hear me. You're nothing but a rotted-out, burned-up old Indian."

Rick Overlooking Horse didn't bother to look up. He hung up the last of his shirts and went inside his teepee.

He could hear You Choose revving his engine and kicking up mud, screaming and shouting. His pickup sounded like it was about to blow a piston, and he himself sounded drunk.

"You're a freak," You Choose What Son shrieked. "You should see yourself. Look in a mirror sometime!"

Rick Overlooking Horse burned sage and smudged his

hair with smoke. Then he lay on the buffalo hide with his hands over his chest.

"I'm not done here," You Choose was shouting. "I'm gonna get ya! You melted-down old cripple. I'm gonna finish ya!"

Everyone knows that for rage to die it has to be left alone in the middle of nowhere, on stony, dry ground. Although the bigger the rage, the longer it will take to die, and the more likely someone will come along and feed it before it is quite dead.

Meantime, rage will get by on scraps. And rage has no problem lying dormant for generations, fasting, if need be.

Which is why forgiveness is such a trick. What events do we forgive? And who decides, lest we forget? Forget what, and whom?

And what if forgiveness looks like all energies of destruction sucking suddenly inward, so that instead of a naked, screaming girl running from a rain of ruin the *Time* magazine photographer captures images of a villain unclothed and burning?

Time, being what it is, it's only a matter of time.

You Choose What Son's Very Vigorous Rage

In any case, memory wobbles and floods. And how we remember has largely to do with everything else in our lives. In the case of You Choose, it was as if everything that had happened to him—or failed to happen to him—turned toxic in his brain, flooded his veins with urgency, set fire ants swarming on his skin.

"I'll be back for you!" You Choose screamed. He fired a few shots in the air.

Afterward, he said he could not remember being at Rick Overlooking Horse's teepee. Or firing off the shots that several people reporting hearing. Nor, he said, could he remember driving back into Pine Ridge village, parking in front of the old tribal government brick house on First Street, pouring gasoline over the contents of the house, and burning the whole place to the ground.

No one believed him, of course. No one believed he could forget doing *that*. No one believed him either when he said he could not remember running into the little white Baptist Church on the road to Wanblee with his gun. He shot the windows out, fired several rounds into the walls, ran back to his pickup, spun it around, and drove off.

You Choose drove off the Rez altogether after that, racing the two miles to Whiteclay, Nebraska. He piled out of his pickup, ran into the first liquor store he could get into, opened fire, and hurt exactly no one. Although there were cases of beer and a few bottles of Old Crow Kentucky Straight Bourbon Whiskey that would never give any more problems.

Ten years he got for that impressive list of serious offences, with an additional thirty years slapped on for a host of offences he did not commit, but which the district attorney in Rapid City was relieved to be able to pin on someone without the money or connections to defend himself.

The proprietor of the liquor store was back at the cash register a few hours after You Choose What Son was arrested. His concession to heightened security was to board up the windows, behind the bars. It made the liquor store's unnatural greenish fluorescent light an almost exact preview of the light found in prisons, which, in fact, it was for a lot of Indians.

Part

TWO

The Great Fertility Crisis of
Le-a Brings Plenty

If, as they say, everything happens for a reason, Le-a Brings Plenty had no choice but to be experiencing her Great Fertility Crisis at the same time as everything else that needed to happen. Which was *everything* else because, as Le-a had been saying for some months now, she could feel her babies calling to her from the other side.

"They're on their way," she insisted. "I can hear them."

She said this spread out in the back room of Squanto's HUD unit on a bottomed-out sofa, blankets over the window so she couldn't see the white death driving in from the north. There were three pots of water on the stove, billowing humidity. Another pot contained water from Le-a's own body. "Well, I'm sure as hell not going out there to freeze my Red Indian ass off," she said. "You want me to die out there?"

The storm of 1994 everyone was already calling it, although it was still only January and winter had a few months of fury in it yet. Worst winter in fifty years said the Elders, some of whom could still remember the terrible cold of 1944.

Le-a patted her belly. "Hey," she said. "You want to keep me warm, soldier?"

But Squanto was halfway out the front door, wrapped in all the winter clothes he could find over his uniform. "I've got to get to work, Crazy Love."

Not that being a security guard at the Lakota Oglala Sioux Tribal Hospital paid like real work. Still, with unemployment the way it was, and not much else to do on the Rez in the winter except attend to Le-a's Great Fertility Crisis, Squanto was happy to have a reason to leave the HUD unit once a week and wrangle drunks and delusional diabetics at the LOST Hospital.

"In this weather? Are you out of your mind?"

"I'll be back," Squanto promised.

"Squanto, babies don't happen on their own!"

"I know. I know, Crazy Love. But neither do paychecks." Squanto blew Le-a a kiss and stepped outside. The wind slammed the door out of his hands.

"Squanto!"

The 1965
Chevy Impala

Squanto hurried out to the 1965 Chevy Impala, held together with bungee cord, duct tape, and tie wire. He lit the candle in the empty five-pound coffee tin on the passenger side floor for heat, prayed the engine into life, scraped a hole in the ice on the windscreen just enough to give him tunnel vision of the road ahead, and jolted out of the yard, down the hill, past Pinky's Grocery & Supply, letting gravity do the work until he hit the main road.

Then he slipped into third gear and made a calculation that he had enough gas to work four more shifts this week if he slept over at the hospital a couple of nights. Which would give Le-a time to calm the fuck down, or to get wound the fuck up into a real state, one of the two.

Squanto tapped the car radio; then he smacked it. Nothing came from KILI 90.1 FM radio. Then he jiggled wires, and finally the jaunty, familiar voice of Tray Tor Two Bulls came at Squanto, "Well, I ain't got no timepiece, so it's skin-thirty here on the Rez, innit? Stand by for a detailed weather report from our expert meteorological team, coming up next." There was a pause. "Yep, I just looked out the window, and here it is, straight from the Tray Tor's mouth. Lila oh snee, Indians! You cold yet, All My Relations? Because she's only gonna blow colder."

Squanto lit a cigarette and prayed the hill at Wounded Knee wouldn't be blown over. Rezercise, they called it, when your car bottomed out and you had to walk. Squanto shook his head and sighed out a plume of American Legend. The glorious, short life of the Rezzer. If he ever got around to it, he would write a book about it, set the record straight.

Because Squanto believed that the Rez, also known as Prisoner of War Camp #334, also known as the Pine Ridge Indian Reservation, also known as the Oglala Lakota Native American Reserve in the southwest corner of South Dakota was a godforsaken patch of land with the propensity for extreme weather.

But Squanto believed too that the Rez was mysterious, wild, and glorious, and there was beauty and freedom here along with all the poverty and hardship, and sometimes miracles ensued.

Somehow, as they say.

Somehow miracles ensued.

One Common Myth About
the Rez, Dispelled

People who do not know the Rez say it is a complicated place. They are confused by what they do not understand.

The Rez is not a complicated place; it is an essential place.

Essential. Meaning, there is nothing more that can be taken away, removed, or forgotten.

Essential. Meaning, there remains only what is absolutely necessary.

Essential. Meaning, it doesn't get any more real than this.

Le-a Brings Plenty
Gets Many DWIs

The 1965 Chevy Impala was Le-a's and it had taken on many of her characteristics; stubborn, unpredictable, and with a steering mechanism that seemed to work on the basis that it was reluctantly prepared to take suggestions but not much more than that. It was also prone to show up on the wrong side of the White Man's law when you ran the license plate. Although, to be fair, the lawlessness wasn't entirely the fault of the car: For one thing, having inherited the car on her mother's death, there had been no one to give Le-a driving lessons.

The tribal cops, knowing better, mostly stayed out of Le-a's way, but she accumulated tickets in a seven-state area—South Dakota, Montana, Nebraska, Wyoming, North Dakota, Iowa, Minnesota—tickets that sat in a yellowing, unpaid pile on the dashboard. "My DWIs," Le-a called them, "Driving While Indian," and she sure as shit wasn't going to cough up a dime for that maggoty-assed, trumped-up, genocidal, nonoffence.

Of course, Le-a had her license revoked, then canceled altogether, which didn't stop her driving. "I don't need a crackerjack's certificate to tell me if I can drive on Native Ground," she said. Eventually, in November 1990, a week after her seventeenth birthday, she'd been arrested at a sobriety checkpoint outside of Rapid City, South Dakota. The state troopers, dipping with Breathalyzers into every car, like huge black butterflies, lingered longest over cars stuffed with Indians.

They found Le-a sober, but without any papers to prove she was legal to drive and even fewer to prove the Impala was legal to be driven. Le-a suggested the sheriff's deputy shove his traffic ticket up his fat, pink, donut-fed ass.

For which Le-a landed herself a driving suspension, and seven months in Pennington County Jail.

Le-a Brings Plenty's
Father Issue

According to Thunder Hawk Brings Plenty, Le-a technically was missing a biological, earthly father. "Just like
Jesus," Thunder Hawk had told her when the child was five
and beginning to ask questions.

Le-a stood in front of the murky mirror in her mother's
bedroom and stared at her face in its reflection. She traced
her nose, her mouth, the way her hair fell. It was true she
looked strikingly like a smaller, rounder version of Thunder
Hawk. It was as if there were nothing of a father's cells or
tendencies or blood inside her. It was as if she had been
cloned straight from her mother.

"Why Jesus?" Le-a asked.

"No special reason," Thunder Hawk said. "But it reminded me, any story about a father that doesn't live with their kid is an unlikely story. It doesn't work in real life to say your Dad's invisible."

The point is, Thunder Hawk explained, no one can tell you who your father is, or is not, especially not the Bureau of Indian Affairs. "If they believe Jesus said he was the son of God, I'm not going to let a bunch of office clerks decide if you're Indian enough for them," Thunder Hawk said. "I've already told them whose blood you have."

"Whose?" Le-a said.

"Mine," Thunder Hawk said. "What more do they want?"

Le-a's Certificate of
Degree of Indian Blood

So, Le-a Brings Plenty's Certificate of Degree of Indian Blood said she was seven-sixteenths Lakota, five-sixteenths Maricopa, and four-sixteenths Pima. But although Le-a got a small check for some federal gravel-mining entitlements down on the Gila River Indian Community, that place was not her home. She knew this because after her mother died of tuberculosis, leaving Le-a an emancipated orphan at the age of fourteen, Le-a headed south in search of nine sixteenths of her people and found those Indians missing a season.

Afterward, Squanto asked her if she'd ever considered going to Palestine to look for her father.

Le-a said, "You mean, I should go all the way over there and track down all the male delegates that attended the Second Annual Meeting of the International Society of Displaced Peoples and ask if any of them slept with a Lakota woman in Ramallah in the winter of 1973?"

"Well, yeah," Squanto said.

Le-a shut her eyes.

You Do the Math

During the Siege of Wounded Knee in the early weeks of 1973, Le-a Brings Plenty's soon-to-be mother was in Palestine on a trip funded by the International Society of Displaced Peoples. Afterward she said it was the best thing she had ever done, and the worst.

Because just for a start, there she was: Thunder Hawk Brings Plenty—an American Indian woman from the Pine Ridge Indian Reservation, no less—whose people were currently sitting in protest at Wounded Knee.

Thunder Hawk represented everything having to do with refugees and internally displaced people. Everyone agreed that a poster child for a cause had never been so striking, so authentic, and so imminently endangered. It was a sudden and unwelcome prominence. Thunder Hawk said over and over, "But I'm not even with my people. I need to be *with* my people."

Thunder Hawk couldn't sleep. At night she paced the streets and watched the strange constellations make their ways across a clear desert sky and she longed for the hearth fires of her own village. She was overcome with an irritable restlessness. Some mornings she awoke to find herself a day's journey from where she had started, with only the haziest recollection of arriving there.

She was certain she was in the process of losing her mind.

One night, she was asked to speak at an event honoring local leaders of indigenous groups around the world. When her turn came, she stood up on the stage and saw a wall of faces staring at her. "I am Thunder Hawk Brings Plenty from the Pine Ridge Indian Reservation in South Dakota. I wish I did not know what I know," she said. "I wish my people were on their land, and that I did not need to be here."

There was a rustle through the audience.

"They can say what they like about what happened to Indians in my land. They can rewrite history, and erase our stories. But what my mind hasn't been allowed to know, my body has always known," Thunder Hawk said. "I am an undeniable, inconvenient body of knowledge. Read me."

And then Thunder Hawk Brings Plenty stood in silence for fifteen minutes in front of her live audience.

Of course, fifteen minutes is not long enough to know the whole undeniable, inconvenient history of the Oglala Lakota Oyate, or even the whole undeniable, inconvenient history of a single Lakota-born woman. But it is long enough for people to begin to know discomfort, and that's a start.

A Secret Is Something You
Don't Already Know

Thunder Hawk kept only one photograph from her time in Palestine. In it, she's standing next to Yasser Arafat on a ramshackle rooftop. There are chickens and a dog with a curly tail at their feet. Thunder Hawk is holding a rifle across her belly. The wind is blowing Yasser Arafat's keffiyeh across her mouth. Behind them, there are a few dusty buildings blazing in the sun, and a narrow two-track dirt road that melds indistinctly into the desert. The sky is the color of a gas flame.

"He's very ugly," Le-a said.

"I ate pigeon with him," Thunder Hawk said. "And camel meat."

"What did it taste like?"

"Salty," Thunder Hawk said. "But also like you'd imagine. Like the smell of camel, which is sort of greasy and gamey. It was a little off-putting at first. But after a while, you didn't notice so much."

Le-a Does Her Time

L e-a nearly drove the corrections officers crazy demanding her religious right to purification ceremonies, and fasting on Thanksgiving Day, "the National Day of Mourning," she called it, and declaring herself a political prisoner. She had a Leonard Peltier quote prison-tattooed on her right arm—"Spirit Warrior"—and the two feathers of the warrior society prison-tattooed on her left arm. And she hollered and yelled her name, the correct pronunciation of it, "You can't read? What's wrong with you? The dash ain't silent. It's Le*dash*a, you asshole. Le*dash*a!"

Then when some well-meaning do-gooders came from the local well-meaning do-gooder society to do arts and crafts with the inmates, Le-a hid little pots of red and black paint under the cover of her orange jumpsuit and after that there were scrawls all over her cell block, the shower block, the rec room: **SACAGAWEA, GUIDING LOST WHITE MEN SINCE 1804; MY HEROES HAVE ALWAYS KILLED COWBOYS; FREE LEONARD PELTIER.** She was put in the Secure Holding Unit for three days after that, and set off the sprinkler system burning sage that she had secreted in places you can't imagine sage might be comfortable.

During those three days in the Shoe, a sock draped over her eyes against the buzzing white light that was never switched off, Le-a Brings Plenty planned her future. There would be dozens of teepees set up in a meadow, and young Indian warriors everywhere, all braids and camouflage. She would be in the middle of them. A Stars and Stripes would be flying from a lodgepole pine, upside down. In accordance with the Flag Code of the United States of America, the flag should never be displayed union down, except as a signal of dire distress in instances of extreme danger to life or property. "You can bet my Red Indian ass I'm in extreme danger," Le-a would say.

When her term was up, Le-a Brings Plenty walked out of the jail gates unbowed, a few pounds lighter than when she went in, her fist raised high. "The Indian Wars are not over!" she shouted.

"Jesus wept," her CO said. "You lost. Get over it."

"Hoka hey!" Le-a yelled back, flipping her CO the bird for a final time.

Then she crossed the road to a phone booth outside the Taco Bell and reversed the charges. "Tell All My Relations to come fetch my Red Indian ass," she told Tray Tor Two Bulls when he took the call. "Put out a broadcast on KILI 90.1. Tell them Le-a Brings Plenty is out of the slammer."

"Le-a, is that you?" Tray Tor asked.

"You bet your scrawny Red Indian ass it is. And oh yeah, tell them Le-a Brings Plenty is looking fine, and she's on the love path. Got that? Love path. Tell them I'm in the market for a soldier."

The Battle of the Junkyard

Although, at first glance, Squanto wasn't most people's idea of a soldier, at least not by any U.S. Army handbook definition of the word. Squanto's entire war was the length of one five-hour, possibly accidental, battle, and he had stopped fighting, or even pretending to fight, about half an hour into it. Maybe even less.

Like just about every battle in the world, the Battle of Rumaila had a few names. Some people called it the Battle of the Causeway, or the Highway of Death, but the name that stuck was the Battle of the Junkyard. Boxed into a kill zone, the several hundred Iraqi vehicles streaming out of the Euphrates Valley toward Baghdad didn't stand a chance. They lay smoldering on their sides, or blasted down to their wheels, draped over with the bodies of their trapped passengers.

Afterward, questions were asked, not least because when

the Battle of the Junkyard happened, on March 2, 1991, the war had been officially over for two days, and formal peace talks were due to take place the following day. Still, if it wasn't an official war, whatever was going on would sure as hell do until one in uniform showed up. Squanto watched the desert burst into black plumes of smoke. When the smoke drifted and cleared he could see men running into the river to swim to safety. Aircraft strafed everything: the sand, the river, and roads.

The Warrior

An Indian makes a good sniper for the following reason: He can lie belly down in the heat and the cold for days, no food, no water, no rest, no shelter. Hamblechya trained you for that, four days and three nights in Rick Overlooking Horse's meadow there on the other side of Porcupine Butte with nothing to look at but a meadow, and Ugly Red Stud, and an old buffalo bull, until your lips split and you started to see yourself in a blade of grass, or in the creatures that feed from it, or in all creation.

In an almost unprecedented fit of loquacity, Rick Overlooking Horse told Squanto, "Remember this: There will be nothing to signal the start of your war. There will be nothing to signal its end. There's just your war. Only you will know it when it has started, and only you can choose when it will end."

At the time Squanto had been so taken aback at the sheer number of words that had come out of Rick Overlooking Horse's snapping-turtle mouth at one time, he hadn't been able to respond.

Now Squanto knew that what Rick Overlooking Horse had said was true. He also knew something else that Rick Overlooking Horse had failed to tell him: That the enemy wasn't his enemy. The ones that could still move were pouring out of their tanks and vans and pickups like ants away from vinegar. Some of them were zinging back the odd, aimless potshot toward the road. But they were not the enemy.

His enemy was the very unit to which he belonged. The Twenty-fourth Infantry Division led by that maniac general ordering his troops to open fire on a retreating column of Iraqis. Hell, even Squanto could see this wasn't anything to fight about. But the war had been a quiet one so far, and maybe that's what had incensed the general. In any case, before you knew it, there were AH-64 Apache attack helicopters streaming overhead and M2 Bradleys roaring into position.

Honestly, what was the point? Squanto heard the Cowboy from Texas in the dugout next to him pop off three more rounds. Three figures running from the burned-out highway jerked forward. Through his sights, Squanto could see what looked like black oil stains spread into the sand around their bodies. Squanto took one last swallow of water and stuffed two packets of cigarettes in his pocket; then he put down his gun and walked out into the battle.

He tore the cigarette packets with his teeth and sprinkled their contents along the road, even though he knew there wasn't enough tobacco in the world to placate all the traumatized, surprised, crossing-over spirits in this hot, terrible place. "Leave this place," Squanto said. "Don't follow us home." And he kept walking like that, sprinkling tobacco and inviting the crossed-over to join his Ancestors in the Great Mystery. "You'll see them," Squanto assured the Iraqi bodies he passed. "All My Lakota Relations."

The Easiest Way to Find
a Warrior on the Rez

The day of the Fifteenth Annual Gathering of Nations on the Pine Ridge Indian Reservation dawned immoderately hot. At the old boarding school near the Red Cloud Cemetery, families without running water in their homes lined up early to fill up containers at the outside faucet. Withholding clouds scudded hastily across the bleached sky, and a seemingly perpetual chorus of grasshoppers sawed a soundtrack of heat.

Squanto put on his full U.S. Army dress uniform for the last time. He walked to the Powwow Grounds on the edge of Pine Ridge village, where kids on horses were wheeling about and showing off, and Chief Oliver Red Cloud, perched on a bale of hay in the back of a pickup, sweated wordlessly under his red and white headdress. A few teenagers set off firecrackers to watch the old war vets startle.

Meantime, on her way from Manderson village, Le-a Brings Plenty had seen a snapping turtle in the middle of the road, dried slime from the creek still on its back. She had stopped for it, and it stopped for her, and they waited like that for half an hour, watching each other, while the sun burned stitches into the earth. No other cars came, but two boys, bareback on Indian ponies, jogged by on the verge.

By the time she got there, the Powwow Grounds already smelled of crushed grass, sweating horses, and Mexican food. Le-a set up her fry bread and stew stand opposite the entrance to the arbor, the better to see everyone coming in. At last, well past the advertised time of one o'clock, the heat bleaching everything pale yellow by now, Chief Red Cloud rose to his feet stiffly and announced that the Wiping of the Tears Ceremony would begin. "All My Lakota Relatives," he said.

He cleared his throat into the microphone to ensure he had people's attention. There's nothing like an old Indian with something to say first in Lakota, then translated by himself into English, but at last taps were played for all the Indian servicemen and women who wouldn't be coming home, and their names were read aloud, one by one.

There were a lot of them.

In fact, it felt to Le-a that there must be more war-dead

Lakota than could be statistically possible, and the weight of all those cut-short lives mixed with the humidity and heat to cast a feeling of absolute melancholy over the arbor. But then Chief Red Cloud gave the signal and a shout went through the ranks massing at the entrance to the arbor.

Le-a sat up.

There were still a handful of soldiers from the Second World War, a lot of them a bit doddery now, their guns wavering. The ranks swelled when Vietnam and Korea came up. But those men too looked like their best years were behind them. Even the legendary Evelyn "Eddie" Two Eagles, who had flown a hundred and ten combat missions over Vietnam and been awarded eight Air Medals and two Crosses of Gallantry, was looking shrunken in his uniform.

Le-a sighed and crossed her arms. And then she saw him, Squanto, three men deep in the Desert Storm contingent. He looked lost, or put another way, like a man needing to be found. He certainly didn't look as if he'd tried anything too horribly, violently heroic in his life.

"Ah, there you are," Le-a said. "I've found you."

Le-a's Other Men,
and One Woman

Before Squanto, there were four men she did not choose: A youth minister from Minnesota, a couple of so-called Rez uncles, and a drunk outside the public toilets one night at the Powwow. And there were six men that she did choose, more or less: A Cowboy from Chadron, a half-blood Cherokee basketball player from Georgia, an aging Lakota AIMster, a German tourist, an Asian American ponytailed University of Texas anthropologist, and an unemployed White carpenter from Kansas.

The year she turned fifteen and was off the Rez for a while, there had also been an Indian girl in Scottsbluff fresh off a week of ICU suicide watch, cartwheeling drunk on a humid September night. Le-a was half wrecked herself, tumbling earthward and skyward on a creaking swing in a school playground, when the girl's mouth connected briefly to hers, teeth bringing a salty shot of blood to Le-a's tongue.

"You're tall for a Lakota," Le-a said.

"Yeah, they say there was also some Karankawa blood way back."

"Some who?"

"Stretched-out Texas Indians. What about you?"

"I don't know," Le-a said. "Mostly Lakota, I guess."

Later that night, camped out behind a gas station west of the Nebraska/Wyoming line, Mona straddled Le-a and declared, like war, "I want to eat you alive." Le-a believed her, the way Mona's breath was fuel scented with unmet need. So she pulled her knees up and said, "Get off of me."

But Mona was dug all the way into Le-a, and breathing heavily. "You're the only person who's ever wanted me," she said. The girls made love then, or something like it, until finally Mona slept. Just before dawn, Le-a gathered her belongings, snuck into the gas station bathroom, and washed herself in the sink. Then she stood by a gas pump until a farmer on his way back to Nebraska agreed he'd give her a lift to the Rez border.

"I'm part Indian myself, you know," he said.

Le-a pulled herself into the cab, weary beyond imagining. "Oh yeah," she said. "Which part?"

The last Le-a saw of her, Mona Respects Nothing was a crumpled bundle on the grass behind the gas station. From a distance, Mona looked discarded, like something pulled from the rotting piles of secondhand clothes that were sent out to Pine Ridge every summer. Then the sun spilled light around the edge of the flat, beige, cinder-block buildings; bail bond shops, nail salons, fast food outlets. And Mona was gone. Le-a closed her eyes and slumped back into the passenger seat.

"Done," she said.

"Say again?" the farmer said.

But Le-a didn't repeat herself. She was done repeating herself and she was done repeating the sorrow of too many generations. Done, done, done.

What Happened Next

The belief that we can be done with our past is a myth. The past is nudging at us constantly. Not only our own pasts, of course, but also the pasts of our ancestors. And the pasts of people we've never even heard of, and to whom we are not related at all. The energies of their great passions hang in the air forever, and possess a forever half-life, and all of that is awash in the universe.

To believe in the doneness of time, and in the doneness of acts committed in that time, is wishful thinking. The truth is, no one is ever done with the past, any more than it is possible for anyone to be done with the future. Months, years, decades, centuries—the sins of the fathers, the mothers, the others, the selves—they wash into now, and into the future, and there is no stopping them.

In this way, it is best to think of time more as the sea,

washing out, and in; out and in; out and in. Yes, you can throw your garbage into the sea, but eventually the used toothbrushes and bottles and plastic lighters and spent condoms will wash up on the beach. Not your beach, maybe, but someone's beach.

So imagine that the only escape from this torture is the same as saying that from this point on, the whole world must agree never to throw anything into the sea again, ever. We'd still have generations having to clean up the beaches. Even if we stopped everything right now, all the war and abuse and hurt and injury, and treated one another with nothing but love.

We'd still have generations to go before we settled into real peace, but it would be real peace.

The question isn't "Why bother?"

It's "Why not?"

Perhaps the answer is that most people don't believe in themselves enough to imagine one or two or seven generations down the line, the way the Lakota are trained to think. Perhaps they refuse to entrust the possibility of peace to some as yet unborn descendants because their own ancestors showed no such respect for their possibility of peace, and so on. An eye for an eye in ever-increasing cycles of violence going all the way around to where this all ends, and all begins.

Mona Respects Nothing
Comes to Whiteclay

The middle-aged man from Florida with sour blue eyes and the thin grey ponytail liked to claim Seminole somewhere down the line. But the Indians called him the Small Nosebleed Indian, because they said a mild hemorrhage from a single nostril would be all it would take to get rid of every last drop of his native blood.

And because they were Indian, and fond of nicknames, they also called him Tío Sopa Vómito because he grew a thick black mustache like a Mexican drug lord, and ran a makeshift soup kitchen for drunks in Whiteclay. It was a gloomy, dingy place. It smelled of rancid animal fat and stale urine. But the Small Nosebleed Indian acted like he'd founded the equivalent of Mother Teresa's Kalighat Home for the Dying Destitutes.

"Be safe with me," he implored the drunk Indians.

The Indians didn't much like getting hauled indoors by Tío Sopa. For one thing, he liked to pray over them, his voice rising like a red tide, and just as suffocating. For another thing, as long as they were under his watch, the Indians felt it was only polite to leave their liquor and each other alone, and that was an abrupt and unpleasant way to come around. So a lot of times the Indians insisted they were okay—"No man, we're just fine like we are"—and waved Tío Sopa away.

"I hate these people more and more each day," Tío Sopa muttered. "How can you help people who refuse to help themselves?"

But as she blew unsteadily into Whiteclay on that frozen afternoon at the onset of the storm of 1994, Mona Respects Nothing was a vision of need; her lips blue, her eyes glazed, icicles across her cheeks. Tío Sopa swept up against her, arms around her shoulders. "You must come in out of this cold. You'll die out here. Come with me." And then he noticed that the woman was not only very drunk, she was also vastly pregnant, and moaning to herself. "Oh, Christ's work on the cross!" he said. "How did you get like this?"

"Help me!" the woman pleaded.

He said, "What did you think would happen?" But he supported Mona to the soup kitchen where he kept an old sedan, battered and rusted. He pushed the woman into the backseat, and cursed at the engine to start.

"Stay alive!" Tío Sopa shouted, which was perhaps the

right thing to do, because Mona's lungs shocked full of air. "Don't die on my watch," he said. Then he drove eight miles to the Lakota Oglala Sioux Tribal Hospital faster than you would think a former cocaine addict from the Sunshine State with one drop of Seminole Indian blood and bald tires should drive on blowing-sideways snow and black ice.

Mona Respects
Nothing Delivers

The first baby came in a hurry. The nurse, who had seen enough of everything in her years with the Indian Health Services, recognized immediately that he was a child of a rudderless woman. She sighed when the baby shuddered and began to whimper. "Hau," she said, turning the child over and wiping mucus from his mouth. "Tanyán yahí," she said, trying to sound as if she meant it. "It's good you came."

She washed the baby in warm water and sage, wrapped him in a towel, and tried to hand him to his mother. "Hoke she la hay cha," she told Mona.

"Jerusalem," Mona whispered.

"What did you say?" the nurse said.

"Jerusalem," Mona said. "His name."

The nurse said, "You'll have time to think about it. After you've had a chance to sober up, maybe."

But suddenly Mona started screaming again.

"Shhh, it's all over," the nurse said.

Mona screamed louder.

"What's wrong with you?" the nurse said. "It's all over. You're okay."

But Mona grabbed the edges of the mattress and rocked back and forth, as if trying to escape the confines of her body. "There's another one!" she shouted.

"No, no, there isn't," the nurse said firmly. "It's just the afterbirth." She bit her lip. She hated the drunk ones forced suddenly dry. Everything about them, she hated: Their smell, their demons, and their terrors, to say nothing of their better-off-dead babies.

"Help me," Mona begged.

"Okay," the nurse said. "You're gonna be okay. But you're withdrawing real fast, and you're dehydrated. I'll get you an IV as soon as I can find a vein."

But Mona, wracked with another spasm, swiped at the nurse violently. She screamed again. Then she bore down, and suddenly another baby shot into world.

"Oh, ho-lay!" the nurse said.

A tiny, blood-streaked creature the color and apparent texture of melted white paraffin candles lay still between Mona's legs. "Oh," the nurse said. "No. Oh. No." But the baby gave a spluttering cough. The nurse grasped the baby's feet and held him upside down. It was another boy, although this one was so small and such an unlikely waxy shade of white he looked more like a deep underwater creature brought unkindly, and too fast, to air.

"Did you know you were having twins?" the nurse asked.

"Daniel," Mona whispered.

"We'll have time for the Naming Ceremony," the nurse said. "Later." She stared down at the baby, its ankles thin as pencils in her fingers.

Afterbirth

I t was dawn before the nurse had a chance to put her feet up and smoke a cigarette on the bed in the back room. She ached from leaning over the babies, and from caring for the various ailments of their embattled mother. The effects on the pelvic floor of a hasty vaginal delivery of twin boys could be dramatic, but in the nurse's opinion, were the least of Mona's problems.

The nurse waved her cigarette at Squanto. "What's the point of one more unwanted child? Let alone two."

"Maybe she wants them," Squanto said.

"She doesn't want them. She doesn't even want her own self," the nurse said.

"I guess everyone's born for a reason," Squanto said.

The nurse shot Squanto a look, dropped the end of her cigarette into an empty Pace Salsa jar, screwed the lid on, and shook it dead. "You can't really believe that," she said. "You can't believe some people were born for any reason other than a very fucked-up one. A lot of fucked-up shit happened, and then a baby or two was born. Then a lot more fucked-up shit happens. That's how it goes in my experience."

Post-Delivery DTs

While the winter storm raged on outside, Mona lay in bed plummeting into sobriety, alternately boiling and freezing, hallucinating dancing heyokas in all their spidery, scary holiness. Between fevers she put a pillow over her ears, to drown out the sound of the twins. Her milk did not come in. The nurse tried to encourage her to feed her babies, change them, and bath them. But Mona looked stunned, as if this life she was experiencing should have been happening to someone else, in some other place.

Then on the third day, Mona said she felt better and needed to wash.

So Squanto held the twins in the nurse's makeshift bedroom while Mona took a shower.

"Everything's going to be okay," he told the boys.

"No, Squanto," the nurse said. "Everything's not going to be okay."

Dallas, the Soap Opera, and the Rez

The nurse watched *Dallas* in endless loops, beginning to end, and then straight back to the beginning again, as if they might have a surprising, hidden answer to all her questions.

"You see," the nurse said to Squanto. "Look at her, that one. It's so obvious," the nurse waved her cigarette at the screen. "You can tell the moment she shows up, she's gonna be trouble."

"Who?"

"Kristin," the nurse said. "Remember? Sue Ellen's sister."

"No," Squanto said.

"She's Sue Ellen's sister. But she has an affair with J.R. And Sue Ellen is J.R.'s wife. Then Kristin shoots J.R. But you don't know it's her. So there's the whole 'Who shot J.R.?'

back and forth. But J.R. doesn't press charges because she says she's pregnant with his baby."

"Huh," Squanto said.

"I know," the nurse said. "And that's not even the best part. The whole of the ninth season turned out to be a dream of Pam Ewing's. Imagine all the people who sat through that without knowing. How messed up is that?"

Everything Is Not Going
to Be All Right

Then Squanto looked at the clock and said it was at least five hours over time for him to be getting home to Le-a because her Great Fertility Crisis meant the longest Squanto could be away from her was about four days, max, and not the wrong four days either.

It snowed. The babies slept. They watched another episode of *Dallas*.

After that, Squanto said it didn't look like his replacement was coming, but if he didn't get home soon, Squanto's life would be over for good and then there would be no LOST Hospital security guard, not one. The nurse and Squanto laughed about that.

Then the nurse noticed Mona Respects Nothing was missing.

Squanto thought to look in the parking lot. Swirling white ground blizzards skated on black ice where car tires had recently pressed tracks into the snow.

"Oh, shit," Squanto said.

"Okay, I'll call the tribal cops," the nurse said. "We don't need a bunch of troopers looking into this shit-upon-shit we're all in right now. Let's keep this Indians taking care of Indians."

Mona Respects Nothing at the Broken Two-Mile Marker

The tribal cop from the Pine Ridge station assessed the situation—the 1965 Chevy Impala resting on a woman's neck where she'd been thrown facedown into the snow at the broken two-mile marker northwest of Pine Ridge village—and radioed for backup.

"No hurry," he said. "We ain't saving a life here. Nothin' that won't keep."

Theo Lone Tree couldn't think how they'd ever separate the woman from the metal. He pulled a pouch from his pocket and sprinkled tobacco around the scene. "Don't look back," he told the spirit of the dead woman. "Don't look what you done." Theo thought about dusting the snow from

Mona's face to get accident-scene photos, but there are some expressions you never want to see.

He radioed his little brother, who was manning the till at Big Bat's. "Anyone there know how long we're in for this weather? I think I got a long night ahead of me." But he really just wanted to talk to someone until the backup arrived. "She's pretty much the deadest thing I ever seen."

That's how news got back to Squanto via the nurse via Tray Tor via Theo Lone Tree's little brother manning the till at Big Bat's: The woman who had stolen Le-a's 1965 Chevrolet Impala from the tribal hospital parking lot wasn't just missing.

She'd crossed over.

The Famous Indian Rescue of Jerusalem and Daniel Respects Nothing

The nurse threw together a bag of supplies—some formula, diapers, a couple of stained but clean premie gowns—and put it at Squanto's feet. "You better get yourself out of here before Theo and them show up and start asking questions," she said.

"Oh no, I ain't taking these babies," Squanto said.

"Oh yes, you are," the nurse lit a cigarette. "Jesus, Squanto, this is no time to spazz out."

"We're okay with kidnapping?" Squanto asked.

"And State of South Dakota Child Protection Services isn't? What do you think is going to happen to these babies if you don't take them?"

"What if her family comes for them?"

"Well, we both know about that," the nurse said. "Holy shit, Squanto, whose side are you on?"

"Le-a will kill me."

"She'll kill you if you don't. I'm dialing Tray Tor Two Bulls right now."

"No, Chaytan. I need time to think," Squanto said.

"About what?" the nurse said. "About the fact you're happy to let these babies die with total strangers. Not on my watch, you don't." Then she turned her attention to the phone, "Tray, that you? It's Chaytan Cedar Face up at the hospital. Listen, húnka, we need help. O ma key ya nah."

Tray Tor and Squanto Are in Charge of Two Very Small Babies for Less Than Three Hours

Tray Tor shut down KILI 90.1 for the night. "All My Relations," he said, "this is your friendly broadcaster closing the Red Sound down for the night. I'll be back when I'm back. Until then, you tune in to you." He drove down from the hill in his 1974 Ford Ranger with its two hundred and fifty thousand miles on the clock. Chaytan Cedar Face piled Squanto and the twins in the passenger seat and Tray Tor turned the heat on as high as it would go, which was blowtorch hot.

"Roads are very quiet," Tray Tor said. "So we got that going for us."

He eased the Ranger out into the road. "Can you see any damn thing?" he asked. "Any trees? Anything at all?" Tray Tor wound down his window a crack. "Also, you're breathing like a fuckin' hunting dog," he told Squanto. "Stop damn breathing. I can't see for damn shit." He rubbed the windscreen vigorously and the Ranger slid, gripping the thicker piles of snow that had accumulated on the leeward side of the road.

Squanto said, "Could you drive properly? I'm holding babies."

"This ain't so easy."

Squanto prayed the Ranger wouldn't get stuck with its bald tires and loose steering and intermittent clutch. He prayed the babies wouldn't freeze to death right there in his arms. He prayed there wouldn't be cops of any sort out in this weather.

What a fucking Rezzed-out way to die.

Tray Tor groped in his shirt pocket then lit a cigarette.

"Now what are you doing?" Squanto said. "Holy shit, don't smoke in the car. These are very sick babies! Stay on the road!"

"Fuck," Tray Tor said and flicked his cigarette out the crack in his window. The pickup fishtailed. "Fuck," Tray Tor said again.

Then the twins started crying and Squanto said, "Now look what you did. You scared the babies."

"It ain't me," Tray Tor said. "It's you that's holding them. Probably you're holding them all wrong."

"I ain't holding them all wrong."

"Then why're they hollering like that?"

"I don't know," Squanto said.

"I do," Tray Tor said. "They don't like the way you're holding them."

"They're scared shitless of your driving," Squanto said. "Fuck Tray Tor, they're nearly dead already."

The 1974 Ranger fishtailed again.

"Fuck, fuck, fuck," Tray Tor said, the steering wheel whipping through his hands.

"Fuck, fuck, fuck," Squanto said.

Part

THREE

The Ugly Red Stud,
at Last

The same winter storm that blew Mona onto the Rez to deliver her sickly boys also blew the Ugly Red Stud to the far edge of Rick Overlooking Horse's meadow. Away from his herd, the Ugly Red Stud turned his back to the wind and let his head hang. His red tail streaked between his legs. The blood stilled in his haunches.

If Rick Overlooking Horse had seen fifty winters, the Ugly Red Stud must have seen thirty at least, most of them hard and long. By January it was clear he didn't have the rest of the freezing season's worth of fight left in him. His ribs hung off his spine like coat hangers. His knees buckled when he walked, especially on cold, hard ground. He avoided the steep trail that led from the meadow up to the exposed grazing along the bluffs.

The Ugly Red Stud fell during the third night of the big storm.

By morning his carcass was hopping with scavengers.

Vigil

Through the obscuring veils of snow swirling from both sky and ground, Rick Overlooking Horse saw the shadowy dance of magpies and ravens at the end of the meadow, and realized what must have happened. He ran out of the teepee, the ground tipping away from him in the dizzying ground blizzard, shouting and waving his arms. "Hey choon sh nee yo! Hee ya! Hee ya!"

Magpies and ravens clattered into the meadow, and hopped about on the snow awkwardly. A coyote trotted off to within what she calculated to be a stone's throw, and then lay on her belly, her chin on her paws, observing the man. Rick Overlooking Horse laid both his hands on the Ugly Red Stud's side. Then he sank slowly into the snow, his face buried in the creature's salt-smelling coat.

There is no word for "good-bye" in Lakota, only, "Doksa ake waunkte." Meaning "I will see you again, later." Since all things are connected, always and for all time, there is no avoiding reunion.

Tray Tor Two Bulls
Seeks Refuge

In Rick Overlooking Horse's dream, there were tunnels everywhere, and inside everything.

He looked up, and saw the sky was a warren of white tunnels, made of clouds.

There were also blond tunnels in the meadow, knitted from dead grass.

There were chalk tunnels underground, carved from clay.

There were yellow and brown wooden tunnels in trees.

Rick Overlooking Horse looked down at his body and saw that it too was riddled with red tunnels, carved from his own flesh.

It was as if all nations were preparing for war.

The air was humming with urgency, and violence.

Rick Overlooking Horse sat up.

There was shouting. It was getting closer. "Oh ma key yo!"

"Huh!" Rick Overlooking Horse replied, standing up.

"Omakiya po!" a man shouted.

Rick Overlooking Horse pulled on a shirt and jacket. "Huh!" he shouted again.

"Rick Overlooking Horse!" Tray Tor Two Bull's head appeared between the flaps of the teepee's entrance. "Ee nah x nee yo!" Tray Tor was breathless. "We have two babies. Weak as kittens."

Ready to Move

It's good and bad, and it says a lot if you, and most of the people you know, are prepared at any moment to leave where you are, with nothing more than what you might be able to carry, and to never look back.

It says a lot if loss is something you're born knowing how to do; and something you've honed with years of practice.

You can't have dark without light.

You can't know wisdom without suffering.

You can't insist on a life. A life insists on you.

The Lakota know this: Let go of everything that was not meant for you.

Le-a didn't look back.

She didn't even shut the door to Squanto's HUD unit.

When the kid from next door came over with a message via Chaytan Cedar Face that orphaned twin Indian baby boys had been delivered to the teepee in Rick Overlooking Horse's meadow, there wasn't a weapon in the arsenal of any army in the world that could stop Le-a from getting to them. "My babies," she said, blundering out into the snow.

The kid stood on the step and watched Le-a disappear. "Shit," he said.

It was a blizzard like you hear tell people die in, and there was Le-a wading through the snow in nothing more than the clothes she'd been in when the kid from next door had burst into the HUD unit with the news.

Exactly as Squanto had told Tray Tor she'd be.

"She'll be north of the junction by now," Squanto said. "And she won't be dressed for this weather. You got to get back out there, Tray. She's gonna be near outta her mind."

So for the second time that night, Tray Tor took the 1974 Ford Ranger out onto the black ice, blown white roads. He thought about how when you were an Indian it was always this way. Nothing happened for days on end, just a slow drip of moments of no particular note, and then suddenly everything started to happen at once, like it had gotten tired of all the waiting.

Staying Babies

No one could say what induced the boys to stay, not even Rick Overlooking Horse who watched over them day and night for that first week; dropping warm mare's milk in their mouths; breathing thin tendrils of Wahupta and sage smoke over them; sleeping with them on his body, their skin touching his.

When it was her turn to hold them, Le-a sang to the babies softly, as if trying to incubate them with her voice, "Cante waste hoksila, ake istima. Hankepi ki waste." It was song that soothed anyone who heard it; the old Lakota words so gentle, so optimistic, so peaceful. Go back to sleep, good-hearted boy. The night is good. Go back to sleep.

Out in the meadow, the storm continued unabated for days and days. The wind howled through the emerging bones of the Ugly Red Stud. Coyotes padded through the thick snow from their dens, their eyes partially battened against the storm, yipping and trilling. The snow around the Ugly Red Stud's body turned pink with the stain of blood. But finally, even the hunger of the scavengers could not keep up with the storm, and everything was white, and waiting and silent.

The Moon of Fattening

The earth turned, and the sun grew stronger.

Snow around the teepee became like mashed sweet potatoes, then like kernels of corn, then granular sugar, and finally it melted completely and puddled up in the tufts of last year's old grass. In early April, shoots of grass, fluorescent with youth, emerged from the yellow thatch. The Ugly Red Stud's bones sheltered a crop of fat maggots and on the first really hot morning of the season metallic-sheened blue-bottles erupted from the carcass.

Life returns furiously fast when it can.

Before month's end, spiderlike harvestmen appeared, leggy emissaries from winter's dark soil. After that, small clouds of blue butterflies showed up, coagulating from the sky in fragments. Robins returned and sheltered from spring storms in tangles of cottonwood branches. Then bluebirds descended, flashing iridescent in the meadow; and the tiny wrens with their big songs. Tree swallows postured and dallied in the cottonwoods. Chickadees held noisy counsel, and within days they were gone from their winter meadow to their summer mountains.

Then the mares started to drop their foals, and by the time the little creek was running ice free, all but three of the Ugly Red Stud's mares had colts at their flanks. Rick Overlooking Horse roped the barren mares and brought them down to graze closer to the teepee, where they'd have an easier time of it; elderly matrons, swaybacked, with faraway eyes, and attitudes of resigned patience.

In another two weeks, the cottonwoods were glittering with lime green shiny leaves. The ravens began courting and chuckling along the creek. Redwing blackbirds shrilled from the willows, where their nests held clutches of eggs. Snakes sunbathed on the dark south-facing rocks.

The sun warmed the canvas of the teepee, and lit its interior a warm yellow. Le-a held the babies' tiny faces toward the sun so that they'd always and in all ways be able to find their ways back to this place, and to her.

Rez-Famous Babies

On the Rez, there are two kinds of famous.

There's world famous, like Michael Jackson.

Then there's Rez famous, like Le-a Brings Plenty, famous for her DWIs. Or, Somebody Overlooking Horse, famous for not dying. And Billy Mills, famous for having the community hall in Pine Ridge named after him.

In this way, Jerusalem and Daniel became Rez famous, not only for being born in that winter storm, but also because of their dramatic rescue from the hospital, and their current status as children of Rick Overlooking Horse's meadow.

It seemed everyone on the Rez needed the twins to make it to dry land. Chief Oliver Red Cloud himself took a Monday noon slot on KILI 90.1 to address the Oglala Lakota Oyate about the Miracle of the Twins, first in Lakota and then, translating himself as usual, in English.

"Mitakuye Oyasin," he started. "We are long past the day when we can think, speak, and act as if our ways will be understood, or respected, by anyone but ourselves."

His speech spilled over into the one o'clock show. "We cannot allow our children to be stolen from us any more. We'll have no more Split Feathers from our sacred fire; no more will we allow our children to be raised as Red Shadows in a White Man's world."

Chief Red Cloud probably would have filled the two o'clock show too if Tray Tor hadn't shut the old man down. "Thank you to our esteemed chief, Oliver Red Cloud," he said, sliding his fingers over the controls, "for those words of wisdom. You're chillin' on KILI 90.1," he said. "Here's some tracks to ease the state of your mind. Kick it! Ladies and Rezidents. Keep it Red, keep it real, and keep it on the Ridge."

An Origin Story

Le-a Brings Plenty talks and talks while she rubs oil into the babies' skin and hair. She tells them windblown spore, the kind that make up whole glorious cottonwood forests, are no less deliberate than they are. She says everyone else on Turtle Island has come from somewhere else. But not Jerusalem and Daniel and everyone like them. She says Indians have no real beginning and no real end because their people have been infinitely here.

"Wakan Tanka has never not been. And you never won't be," Le-a Brings Plenty tells the tiny, sickly babies. "You are C'anupa Oyate. You are the deliberate, conscious choice of all your ancestors and you are the ancestors of those who will come behind you. You are meant to be exactly now, exactly as you are."

The babies unfurl a little. Le-a stretches their fingers open, and holds out both of her thumbs so they can grip one each. "See?" she tells them. "It's not all bad. And you are such good babies. Such important babies. Stay here with us for a while."

Preschool for
Indian Babies

In late summer, when the air was easy on young lungs, Le-a puts the babies on a blanket in the meadow among the herd of grazing Indian ponies. "Wanji, núnpa, yámi, tópa," she says, counting the horses. "Wanji, núnpa, yámi, tópa," she sings. The twins stare at the horses' legs and faces. They pull on fat blades of grass, and put leaves into their mouths. "Wanji, núnpa, yámi, tópa," Le-a croons over and over.

Their second summer, the boys hold onto the legs of the barren old mares and learn to walk. Their third summer, the boys are able to scramble onto the mares, and persuade them, by holding onto their manes and flapping their legs like windmills at their sides, to trot reluctantly around the meadow.

Squanto takes them swimming in the water hole where

the creek joins the river. The boys circle the eddy line, and surprise snapping turtles and bellowing bullfrogs. The deep pool burbles, oily, black, old mud stirs up. There's life and decomposing life in everything.

Squanto throws the boys skyward, over and over.

They soar for a few seconds, then come splashing back down into his waiting arms.

Splash!

He takes them berry picking, root gathering, and wood chopping. He shows them how to walk in the shadows to conserve energy in the summer, and to walk in the sun for the same reason in the winter. He shows them how to quench their dry mouths by biting into an aspen-sheltered rosehip, preferably one that has been through a frost.

He shows them how to sleep under a horse for shelter, and how to use a horse as windbreaker, weapon, or shield. He shows them how to make rope from horsehair, and leather from hide. He shows them how to find honey, and collect it. He shows them how to make a fire, and also how to douse one.

Children's Questions, Answered

What happens at the end of the world, Tunkashila?" Jerusalem asks.

Rick Overlooking Horse prods the fire. Sparks spiral up into the teepee's smoke hole. "No one knows."

"Why?"

"No one who has come back from there has told about it," Rick Overlooking Horse says.

"Shhh," Le-a says.

Another few minutes pass.

Jerusalem thinks and thinks. "Why does the moon stay up?" he asks.

"To remind us how little we know," Rick Overlooking Horse says.

There is more silence, except for the pop of the fire.

Finally Daniel asks, "Are you old?"

"Yes."

The wind picks up, and the teepee sways.

The boys nestle under the blanket.

Rick Overlooking Horse lights his pipe. He smokes a little. Then he starts to talk very softly. The boys settle. Le-a turns toward Squanto, and puts her hands around his chest. She closes her eyes.

Rick Overlooking Horse taps out his pipe, refills it, puffs some more.

How Turtle Island
Got Its Name

I n the beginning before this beginning," Rick Overlooking Horse says. "There was another world. But the people in that other world were greedy and violent. Wakan Tanka was unhappy. So he made rain and rain. The earth split apart. Water gushed up through the cracks. Everything was flooded. All of the people and nearly all of the animals were drowned. Only Crow survived."

The fire smolders. Rick Overlooking Horse nudges a fresh chunk of wood onto it. Outside, the old barren mares crop the grass, and from time to time, one of them blows contentedly. A great horned owl hoots his territorial call, and somewhere a distance away, perhaps in the bluffs, another male hoots in reply.

"Crow begged and pleaded with Wakan Tanka to make

her a new place to roost," Rick Overlooking Horse says. "So Wakan Tanka decided to make a new earth out of the mud of the old world." Rick Overlooking Horse stops talking. Then he says, "Are you still awake, good-hearted boys?"

"Yes," Jerusalem says.

"Yes," Daniel says.

Rick Overlooking Horse relights his pipe and smokes a little more, then he prods the fire and continues, "From his pipe bag, Wakan Tanka chose four animals known for their excellent diving skills; the loon, the otter, the beaver, and the turtle. He asked each, in turn, to dive deep beneath the floodwaters to fetch up some clay with which to make a new world."

The wind picks up, and the teepee shudders against the tug. Rick Overlooking Horse talks about how the loon and the otter and the beaver fail to dive deep enough; how they return to the surface breathless and without mud. Then Rick Overlooking Horse says, "Are you still awake, good-hearted boys?"

"Mm," the boys say.

Rick Overlooking Horse says, "So I will tell you the end of the story."

He pulls up the old buffalo hide across the boys' shoulders and continues, "When it was turtle's turn to dive deep into the floodwaters, she was gone so long everyone thought she must have drowned. They thought her lungs must have burst. They thought her shell must have been crushed. But just as they were about to give up, she came back to the surface of the floodwater with mud in her beak, mud in her feet, mud in her shell."

Rick Overlooking Horse says, "Wakan Tanka thanked little Turtle. He thanked her and took the mud, and made it into the shape of land, just big enough for him and Crow. Then he shook two eagle feathers over the mud until it spread and spread, far and wide. And he named the new land Turtle Island in honor of the brave little turtle."

Rick Overlooking Horse puts fresh logs on the fire. He can hear from their breathing that the boys are now asleep; so are Le-a and Squanto. Rick Overlooking Horse lights his pipe and smokes a little more until he too grows sleepy. Then he says his prayers silently, curls his body against the base of the teepee to catch wind from reaching the boys, and sleeps.

You Choose What Son, Out of the Second Rez

Just when You Choose was getting thoroughly inured to his unpleasant predicament, stupefied into submission by the monotonous brutality of prison life—the perpetual stench, the absence of women, the lack of privacy—he suddenly learned that he'd been granted ten years, minus a few months, off his forty-year sentence for good behavior.

Or maybe he got ten years off, minus a few months, because of U.S. government budget cuts. Or maybe his release was the result of a rare clerical error in favor of the Red Man. Or maybe someone finally felt guilty for the extra thirty that had been tacked onto the original sentence, and decided to put things right.

Or righter.

Let's face it, things could never really be put all the way right at this point.

Which in any case made no difference to You Choose What Son, who never really knew why he was suddenly free to walk out of the gates of the El Reno Federal Correctional Institution thirty miles west of Oklahoma City, a window-less building like a munitions factory, out in the flat middle of western Oklahoma.

From the yard, as far as an inmate could see on a clear day, there was nothing but torn, broken, sterilized, leached land. Where there was vegetation, it was more rubble and weeds than grasses and sedges. There was nothing left at all of any truly wild land.

For as far as the eye could see, the ruins of so much imprisonment.

You Choose What Son's
First Days of Freedom

You Choose hopped the Greyhound straight up north, through Kansas to Grand Island, Nebraska. Then he tacked together journeys west on buses and rides. He bought some weed and a nice pinch of cocaine. By the time he reached Scottsbluff, he had just enough money left for the essentials.

At a dive bar not a block from the Greyhound station, he managed to get very quickly drunk on four beers, and exceedingly drunk on six. After seven beers on an empty stomach, he tried to talk a number of women into sleeping with him.

It should be no surprise then that when he rolled back onto the Rez in early August, You Choose had a black eye, a split lip, and a slice missing from across the top of his left ear.

Prison dentistry had not been kind to his teeth. Also, his haircut betrayed him as the victim of an involuntary life.

It's a difficult look for anyone to embody: Recent con, possibly tough guy with a jittery side of PTSD.

That usually got people paying attention.

You Choose What Son
Buys a Way Out

The Rez had gone downhill since You Choose What Son had been tribal chairman, no question. The old café where he'd got his first political support in that historic 1972 election had been torn down. In its place there was a dented shipping container out of which a fat Mexican who apparently called himself Auntie Sioux sold fry bread and bad coffee. There was an infestation of shoddy HUD units in the old meadows around the Powwow Grounds. And the Rez playground equipment, which had apparently been installed and had time to rust in the time You Choose had been incarcerated, looked dangerous, even to an Indian.

Also, You Choose found he knew no one. And no one knew him.

"What Son," he told the cashier at Big Bat's. "I was tribal chairman. Do you people know nothing about nothing?"

The thugs hadn't changed so much, though.

They were as easy to spot now as they had been back in You Choose What Son's time. Instead of baseball caps, plaid shirts, and jeans, the new thugs dressed like kids on television, all tattoos, beanies, baggy camouflage pants, white T-shirts, and chains. But they exhibited the same air of cultivated, aimless, hanging-around-the-fort disaffection and latent menace.

It took You Choose less than half an hour in the parking lot at Big Bat's to figure out where he could buy a gun for cheap, and another week to complete the purchase mostly because there was some disagreement among the supposed dealer's Immediate Relations about who the gun's more or less rightful owner might have been, to start with.

Still, by the end of it, for twenty-five dollars and a case of Colt 45 Malt Liquor, You Choose What Son was in possession of a Hi-Point C9 semiautomatic 9mm pistol. It had a cheap kick, a tacky feel, and sticky action. But at the price, it was a beautiful piece of heat.

The Moons of August

Ask a human being, any human being, the human standing closest to you: What phase is the moon in right now?

Ask her: Is it waxing, waning, gibbous, or crescent?

Ask a prisoner what he misses most about the outside world.

He'll say women, probably, and the feel of grass beneath his feet, perhaps. But he will definitely tell you he misses the moon.

The summer moon on the evening You Choose What Son walked out of the gates of El Reno Correctional Institution was full, and heavy, as if it had been lowered in vats of syrup, or fresh engine oil. It was a moon that looked as if it could succor, or smother.

Within the month, as measured by the White Man in any case, the moon was full and pregnant again. It went against nature and defied common sense. Two moons in a month was not a month. It was two months.

People capable of making the rudimentary mistake of marking a recurring full moon in a single month should not be in charge of pretty much anything else. A decoy moon, the White Man calls it, covering for his blunder. Or a blue moon, a betrayer moon.

This kind of confusion cannot happen in the Lakota calendar. The Lakota follow the moon; they don't force the moons to follow them.

Accordingly, the last two moons of the summer are Warm Moons.

Canpaspapa wi—moon of blackening berries. Wasuten wi—moon of the harvest.

Everything bakes in the summer heat: Sweet, open, and ripe.

Recipe for Berry Stew

Rick Overlooking Horse showed the boys: To make wojapi, you will need enough chokecherry patties to cover the bottom of a bowl, all the huckleberries and whatever other berries you can find. You will need some prairie turnips, for thickening. You will need water, a pinch of salt, and a pot.

Le-a made fry bread.

Squanto cleared a firebreak.

They sat outside until very late and ate the berry stew together.

The horses grew curious and trotted down from the bluffs, gangly and giddy. A waxing gibbous moon rose in the northeast. There were distant bleeds of yellow and blue lightning on the horizon. And there was an ever so slight scent of rain, maybe.

Very few people can remain calm in the eye of such a brewing storm.

The boys got up and started chasing each other around and around the meadow, which put the wind up the horses and got them snorting and racing too. Rick Overlooking Horse leaned forward and poked the fire.

"It's going to rain," Le-a said.

"Not this moon," Rick Overlooking said. "Not yet."

You Choose and the
Other Full Moon

Le-a's mind, trying to put it all together afterward, missed whole pieces.

She'd been harvesting corn, she remembered that, of course. Feeling tired because of the late night, and angry with herself for sleeping in. And she'd been thinking how small the corn was, stunted in this long, hot summer and no moisture, and now the insult of this virga, the gloomy effect of the sun battling through those curtains of rain that never touch the ground.

And then a strange figure seemingly solidified out of the singed pasture at the bottom of the meadow. There had been no sound of a vehicle to announce a visitor. Le-a shaded her eyes and looked. Only then did it register that the person at the bottom of the meadow seemed to be aiming a gun.

Le-a was already moving through the air, counting the shots as they came—seven, in the end—when Rick Overlooking Horse hit the ground. Then she was at Rick Overlooking Horse's side, on her knees, her mouth seeking his tight-melted lips.

"Oh, please be breathing. Please be breathing."

Her fingers were fumbling for a pulse on his neck. "Oh no, please, please, please."

His neck was warm and wet, his eyes still shiny with life, but she knew he was gone.

It was impossible.

Le-a was screaming, "No!"

But there are a lot of reasons a person cannot easily come back from the dead, and seven bullets are seven of them.

You Choose What Son's Near-Death Experience

Le-a Brings Plenty noticed these things: A feather with creamy brown vanes, and a neon orange rachis; rivulets of sweat, silver on Rick Overlooking Horse's brown neck; a green crayon melting in the sun, its wrapper greasy with paraffin wax.

There is nothing so normal as all these normal things at the end of the world, surely.

Le-a leapt to her feet, and turned to You Choose.

"What have you done?" she screamed.

You Choose stared at the ground.

From the cottonwood grove a northern flicker gave a harsh laugh, and drummed.

Le-a hit You Choose as hard as she could.

After that, You Choose could see ground from the perspective of having his face mashed into it. Drops of blood landed on its glittering surface like tiny bombs. He could hear Le-a screaming but her voice appeared to be coming from a great distance, as did the blows of her fist on the side of his face. Several of his teeth were in the dirt already, he was pretty sure of that. He could feel others rattling around in his mouth, salty little stones.

He noticed how dry the grass was, translucent in the sunlight, as if everything might break apart in orange flames.

RICK OVERLOOKING HORSE, 1944–2004

Half the population of the Pine Ridge Indian Reservation showed up for the funeral. The first three days there was also a Catholic priest from St. Jerome's Mission clattering about with his rosary and parchment paper. His hands like large, dry moths, blessing everyone. His words like steam.

Bless, bless, bless.

But after the Catholic priest left, the whole thing turned very Indian.

Many people cut and burned their hair. Except for You Choose What Son. He didn't need to cut his hair. His haircut was already the "Lakota-in-Mourning"–style insisted upon by most U.S. prisons. Also, his scalp was so encrusted with lacerations, swellings, and bruises; it wasn't really something you wanted to take a razor to.

After that they carried Rick Overlooking Horse's body, wrapped in blankets, to the top of the chalky bluffs. Then they tied his body to a scaffold, and lifted the scaffold high off the ground, away from wild animals. Already the coyotes were yipping and singing with the smell of death, and ravens were gargling about in the cottonwood trees.

You Choose What Son
and the Life Sentence

Anger was the fuel that got Le-a up in the morning, and drove her all day. And she kept You Choose in the crosshair of her fury. "Oh no, I'm sure as shit not turning you in," Le-a said. "Although you're gonna wish I did." She waved the Hi-Point C9 semiautomatic at him. "How does this thing work again?" She flicked the safety on and off.

You Choose hiccupped miserably.

Le-a Brings Plenty could think of no better punishment for You Choose What Son than to force him to stay with them, in Rick Overlooking Horse's meadow. "You didn't just kill a man," she told him. "You killed everything they would ever know. You realize that, don't you? You killed their knowledge. Our knowledge. You killed their best chances. You killed all of us."

You Choose flapped his arms up and down a couple of times, as if experimentally, or as if hoping he'd somehow take flight. He was genuinely confused. This was not death row. Death row was in Sioux Falls, South Dakota.

"Suicide Falls," the Indians say. "Minnehaha County."

Feeling Returns

For days, You Choose What Son was catatonic.

Le-a fed him corn porridge every morning. She took him a pipe of Wahupta every afternoon. She figured whatever was wrong with him mostly had to do with a broken spirit, and there was no real shortcut for the repair of a soul.

Once in a while, she kicked him, to see if he could feel anything yet.

"No?" she said. "Didn't feel that? Try this."

Grief is an eroding wind.

After grief has blown through, there is just the bedrock of a person.

Le-a was worn down to her fury; Squanto was reduced to a state of silent watchfulness; the boys reverted to wild creatures; and You Choose was a pillar of numb.

Until suddenly he wasn't; until suddenly he was all feeling.

It was as if he'd been out in the cold most of his life, and now his capillaries were opening with the full stinging shock of everything he should have felt ever. He lay curled up in front of the teepee fire ring, his hands clutched between his clenched thighs, his mouth wide with agony.

"How long are you going to carry on like this?" Le-a asked.

"Ah, this hurts," he gargled.

"Well, how did you think it would be?" Le-a said.

Because in the perennial boot camp of suffering also known as the Pine Ridge Indian Reservation, also known as the Rez, also known as Prisoner of War Camp #334, even a certified idiot knows the only pain a person can avoid is the pain that comes from trying to avoid pain.

Rain

The last two weeks of August a steady, hot, dry southern wind seared the grass into feathery razors. An infestation of grasshoppers sawed loudly through the crackling drought, shredding Le-a's already stunted corn. The squash turned black on the stalk, slow-cooked rotten on the baking ground. The creek slowed to a barely moving trickle of sludge.

Squanto eyed the sky, and considered pushing the horses south to the reservoir, although he'd heard even that was desperate-dry, down to mud they were saying.

Wildfires roared through Hé Sapa, and turned the sky a poisoned yellow.

Everything seemed restless with waiting and thirst and grief.

You Choose still wailed and blubbered. He sniveled and

rocked himself. He shook out his limbs, as if his extremities were on fire.

He was getting on everyone's nerves.

Then on the night of the full moon, the hot night wind suddenly stilled. Everything grew hushed. Horses took shelter in the little gullies. Up on the bluffs, coyotes yapped and cried.

"Fire," Squanto worried.

"Rain," Le-a prayed.

By dawn, threads of moisture licked the horizon. Then those threads thickened to take the shape of thunderclouds. A steady, insistent wind picked up from the west. By evening the whole sky was battleship grey over the blond meadow.

When it came, it was a deluge. The rain lashed; the branches of the cottonwoods clattered and groaned. Water rushed in rivulets past the teepee; the little creek roared and tumbled rocks.

Le-a Brings Plenty
Hears the Voice of Rick
Overlooking Horse

H au," the voice was unmistakable.

Le-a opened her eyes. "Tunkashila?"

"It's just a life."

Le-a sat up. "Tunkashila?"

But the teepee remained a whispering, golden skin around its sleepers.

Le-a edged out from her blankets and out of the teepee.

The earth looked soaked, at once glistening and exhausted, as if recovering from something ecstatic.

"Tunkashila?" Le-a asked again.

She walked around the back of the teepee. The old, barren mares rested their soaked haunches in the fresh, dawn sun. In the cottonwood trees, ravens burbled and clucked. Wet leaves rustled like silk.

Le-a Brings Plenty Buries the Hatchet, as They Say

The closest Lakota comes to the word for forgiveness is kicicajuju, which literally means "to repay for something on someone's behalf." There is no easily translatable word for forgiveness in the Lakota language, because in a culture that values integrity, forgiveness is not something you say, it's something you do.

Le-a went back into the teepee. She stoked the fire, and put the kettle on to boil. She made a pot of coffee and opened a can of condensed milk. She sliced sun artichokes and fried them with duck eggs, sage, and chunks of corn bread.

Then she felt under the buffalo hide and pulled out the gun.

"Crazy Love?" Squanto propped himself up on his elbow.

"Breakfast is ready," Le-a said.

Squanto said, "What are you doing?"

"I've got to bury this fucking thing," Le-a said, ducking out of the teepee.

"Crazy Love?"

You Choose Watson's Very Born-Again Indian Conversion

There are quiet conversions, the gentle arrival at a series of mild spiritual epiphanies. That was how Le-a came to her soul, as if led toward it by imitating the ways of Rick Overlooking Horse until to behave in such a way became practice, and the practice became internal law. Baptism not by consuming fire, but by warm embers.

That was not You Choose What Son's way. He was all fire and martyrdom, like Saul on the road to Straight Street, Damascus.

"I ain't done a real, whole good thing in my life. I see that now. I have lived only for my own selfish needs. That has made my suffering worse. The only way out of suffering is sacrifice," he said all this like he was auditioning to be the youth pastor of a Born-Again minor megachurch.

"Here we go," Le-a said.

But even she had to admit that artificial light is still light.

It's no substitute for real sunshine, but it can show the way out of the dark.

A Good Thing for
an Indian to Know

You Choose said that most of what he knew in the way of personal experience wasn't the sort of thing you wanted to pass along to the youth as an example. But he did tell the boys the one thing prison teaches you is some people are willfully incapable of using a toilet.

You Choose What Son was thinking specifically of a Taco Jockey from El Paso.

"A what?" Daniel asked.

"A Spice Rack," You Choose said. "Mexicles."

"Really?" Le-a said.

Anyway, the point of You Choose's story was that when it came right down to it, that Taco Jockey didn't take a shit. The shit took him. In the end, the Mexican's cellmates complained and complained, the COs had to move him to a dry cell with wire mesh over a drain hole in the floor.

Then there'd been a waiflike Swamp Yankee from Florida. He had acne-scarred skin that gave him an air of wounded tragedy, and he had a predilection for falling in love with all or any of his cellmates. He'd spent much of his cell time crouched in front of the toilet, with his finger down his throat until he blistered the inside of his mouth.

"What no one tells you," You Choose wanted the boys to know, "is that you don't only serve your own time in prison. If you ain't careful, you also serve the time of everyone around you. Overtime."

"Okay," Le-a said. "Enough said here. Enough said."

You Choose Watson,
Indian Activist

It was almost inevitable that You Choose Watson's American Indian awakening be accompanied by a growing sense of American Indian outrage, followed by furious if somewhat haphazard American Indian activism.

The summer the boys were fifteen, You Choose Watson suddenly chained himself to a sobriety checkpoint barrier in Whiteclay in mid-July to protest the sale of alcohol to Indians. What a performance that was. By the time the Nebraska state troopers managed to hack the chains off his wrist, You Choose was faint with dehydration. Although shriveled up like a prune or not, he still had to spend a week in Sheridan County Jail in Rushville, Nebraska.

A few weeks after getting bailed out of there, You Choose What Son was part of an ongoing Indian protest against an oil pipeline in North Dakota. It was something to see, Indians swarming the state troopers on their war ponies, whooping and ululating. And the troopers all having to back up, as the Indians pressed and swarmed.

"I ride for the water!" a girl on the grey mare shouted at the troopers.

"Hoka hey!" You Choose What Son roared, brandishing a trembling fist at a North Dakota state trooper.

They arrested him for that too.

He was an expensive Indian.

Four hundred dollars on average, every time he had to be sprung from jail.

The boys handed over all their earnings from the Indian Races, but it was never more than fifty bucks a shot. Squanto got his job back at the hospital as security guard, three nights a week, and one or two days a week he helped Gordo Gonzales, proprietor of Speedy G's Taxi Service to ferry rides around the Rez. Le-a took her fry bread and stew to every Powwow and charged fifty cents more for her food than the Mexicans did.

"My Indian tax," she called it, even though she knew figuring out how to pay the White Man's bills on a Red Man's wage was an exercise in futility.

But it was like Squanto said: You had to give it a go before you went completely outlaw, because once you were outlaw, there was no going back to the possibility of being a token Indian, or a good Indian, or the poster-child Indian. Once you went outlaw, then you were there, and that's where you stayed.

Daniel and Jerusalem (Don't)
Win a Thousand Dollars

The twins heard about the race at Thunder Basin, Wyoming, via Tray Tor via Theo Lone Tree via the nurse at the Lakota Oglala Sioux Tribal Hospital. The prize money was enough to cover You Choose What Son's legal bills, plus buy Le-a some time off her feet. It'd be an easy thousand, fifteen hundred if they took first, and second, which, Tray Tor figured, they might. "You should do it," Tray Tor said. "Does you good to get off the Rez once in a while."

Jerusalem and Daniel had to ride a hundred miles just to get to the starting line of the three-hundred-mile Thunder Basin Endurance Race across unfamiliar territory, sleeping in a cattle yard on the Wyoming border. And then when they got there, riders from Oregon, Washington, and California with their fresh Arabians were clattering expensively out of trailers.

"Ho-lay," Daniel said.

"Ho-lay," Jerusalem agreed.

There was concern among the race organizers about the fitness of the boys' horses to run, but the White vet declared the Native Americans' ponies sound in spite of their salt-crusted coats. They had hearts like drums and legs like logs, she said, no denying it.

After that, the organizers said how nice it was that Indigenous People had chosen to race here.

That night the boys slept alongside their grazing horses wrapped in thin blankets. A few dozen people wondered if the Indian kids would be trampled to death in the night. Although a few others expressed the opinion that these Rez donkeys—forgive the expression—were too placid to trample their owners. Also, they said, Indians knew how to sleep with animals, like that.

At dawn, the boys rose, washed in the ablution block, and then walked their horses to the starting line and waited. At six o'clock, bareback except for the thin blankets, with nothing between them and their horses' mouths but a length of horsehair rope, the boys took their places in the middle of the competitors.

They left in no particular hurry, but certainly faster than the White riders, who seemed attached to the race's beginning. Then fifty miles into the ride, just as the day's heat began, the boys found a tiny lush meadow in the cool shade of a stand of quacking aspens near a shallow spring. They dismounted, drank deeply from the spring, and rubbed their horses dry with knots of grass. After that, they slept while their horses grazed.

The other riders clattered ahead out into the long open meadows of sage, past the gloomy aspen grove where the boys rested. Hours later, at dusk, they mounted their horses and jogged, slowly at first, toward the very distant line of headlamps of the other riders picking their way on the steep and winding trail ahead.

On a steep downhill, one that fell away from a cliff, they took flight past all the other riders.

Daniel first, lying almost flat against his horse's back, hands flung above his head for balance, legs stretched out around the horse's shoulders.

Then Jerusalem.

"Hoka-hey!" the boys hollered.

After that, the four souls carved their way through the darkness. The drumming of bare hooves on flinty ground, the percussion of breath, branches whipping.

By the time the boys arrived at the finish line a full day ahead of everyone else, the organizers had been able to find at least three reasons to disqualify them.

"But do stay and join us," they urged. "For the pizza. We always have a pizza party after the race. It's tradition."

Wanted: A Job for Indians

People talk a lot about drunk Indians, unemployed Indians, welfare Indians. They say head onto the Rez any time of the year, and you see squalor and filth.

People ask, "Who lives this way?"

They say, "Who sits here and rots like this? Wouldn't they rather assimilate? Wouldn't they like a job?"

The summer the boys turned eighteen, the only people with jobs on the Rez were soldiers, tribal cops, Catholic priests, and undercover Drug Enforcement Agency narcs.

You could tell the narcs because of their too-shiny kicks. No one has shoes like that on the Rez. Everyone is so goddamned, bottomed-out poor. There're a lot of Indians that don't make one soaking-wet red cent from one winter to the next. Not one cent.

Television crews out of Washington and New York came

onto the Rez and filmed segments about the violence and the gangs and the diseases. They showcased all the HIV, TB, diabetes, cirrhosis, and rape they could find. They talked about alcoholism, and black mold. Men and women were dying like flies. Like Haitians, they said.

The Rez lost its wild promise for the boys. Or maybe there'd never been any promise except for the broken, damaging kind.

The summer turned sullen and sad and oppressive.

It was all those things the television programs said. It was the false starts, and the no starts, and the dead ends that got into the souls of the boys. It was the broken past, the stagnant present, and the unhopeful future.

It seemed the only way to survive on the Rez was to leave.

Leave until you could afford to come back and live so close to such an unforgiving wind.

Ride this current wrong, and there was no going back out for a do-over. You were liquid spill on aisle six.

The Recruiter

There are a lot of Styrofoam Indians on the Rez, who don't know their souls from a bar of soap. There are a lot of drunks on the Rez, let's face it. There are a lot of people half dead on drugs and abuse. So you can't always believe what you hear.

People were saying there was a recruiting officer from Canada for Disneyland France on the Rez. They said he was looking for two real Indian boys for Buffalo Bill's Wild West Show. Everyone said you knew what *that* meant. There'd be a German pimp on the other end of that string. Why not? German women were obsessed with the Lakota men. Why wouldn't German pedophiles be obsessed with Lakota children?

But in the end, when he came door-to-door, the recruiting officer for Disneyland France turned out to be not a teepee-creeping German pimp, but an ordinary enough Cowboy from Calgary who had spent most of his career playing a chuck-wagon Cowboy and also Benjamin Pontipee in *Seven Brides for Seven Brothers*.

Of course, everyone said, he might still be a pimp, but at least he wasn't German.

The Audition

The recruiter was very careful to point out a highlighted section of the contract: "The successful applicant [henceforth known as the applicant] will maintain the appearance of a stereotypical Lakota male youth. He will maintain a full head of hair of at least 30.48 centimeters [one foot] in length from the nape to the point of the skull."

Half a dozen Indians were weeded out right off the bat.

First the fat kids and the kids with short hair were sent away; also, the blatantly fetal-alcohol syndrome kids; then, the wannabe gangsters who showed up with pants too baggy at the ass. And a few kids were dismissed under suspicion of being under the influence of intoxicants. Finally, only six kids were left to show off their real Indianness to the chuck-wagon Cowboy from Calgary.

"Cowboys and Indians," the recruiter said. "Comprendo?"

The Youth of Today

When the boys came home with signed contracts from Disneyland France, Le-a Brings Plenty blamed You Choose What Son for racking up White Man's bills. She accused him of encouraging the boys to be such Feather-duster Indians in the first place.

She blamed him for all of it. "You brainwashed the boys."

"I taught them how to be proud Lakota."

"So how are they now Disneyland Indians?" Le-a shouted.

"The boys need to head off the Rez and see the world for themselves," Squanto said. "We all did it."

"I only headed off the Rez because they arrested my Red Indian ass. I had to be dragged off this place."

"What about Arizona?" You Choose asked.

"Don't bring up my Pima people!" Le-a shouted. "My Maricopa! They have nothing to do with any this! They were minding their business in Arizona."

The argument swirled around and around the teepee, Le-a and You Choose hurling accusations at one another, Squanto trying to remind everyone that nothing was forever. The boys fled and rode horses above the meadow, chasing through the pines, and the white, dusty ribs of the bluffs where the herd grazed in the winter.

Squanto was half right.

Nothing is forever.

But so is everything.

Marne-la-Vallée

Twenty miles east of the center of Paris there's a new town built in the Paris Basin where once there were fields of wheat, oats, rye, and lavender.

Marne-la-Vallée, they called it when mapping it out in 1965, as if inviting a flood.

A modern town hastily built in a river valley that was once covered in peach and apricot orchards; fields of tomatoes and onions, now the headquarters of a large French airline.

There's the Val d'Europe Shopping Center.

Employment!

Designer clothes at outlet prices!

Also, Disneyland Paris, the most visited resort in Europe!

The towers of the Enchanted Palace rise medieval and pink out of a hill that was once good roosting for pheasants.

The Big Thunder Mountain with its Colorado-inspired

redstone cliffs, and artificially rickety Rocky Mountain-seeming cabins, loom over a greenish pond where there'd been, within living memory, some of the best rabbit shooting in the whole of the Paris Basin.

A famous restaurateur in the 6th arrondissement was said to have died of a broken heart when the first bulldozer dug into the earth where he'd harvested rabbits for his kitchen since boyhood. Either that, or all the butter and strong cigarettes finally did in his arteries.

Nonetheless, fucking Americans.

Buffalo Bill's Wild West
Show, Disneyland Paris

First Goofy, Mickey and Minnie Mouse, and Donald Duck dance around a covered wagon. A campfire flickers. Actually, it's a hologram of a campfire. Goofy, Mickey and Minnie Mouse, and Donald Duck dance around the hologram of a campfire. They sing, and encourage the audience to join in. In the background a sunset pulses.

Then Goofy and everyone skip out of the arena, and the music becomes somber, a bit like the sort of pompous military marches favored by South American dictators circa 1975. In a puff of dry ice, Buffalo Bill rides into the ring on a showy dappled grey gelding, all leather fringe and silver fastenings. The sunset goes crazy; purple, pink, yellow!

In real life, Buffalo Bill is Robert "Bob" Davies, a logger from Sandpoint, Idaho. But he grew up riding horses, and everyone always said he was a dead ringer for Buffalo Bill. Plus, keeping a waxed mustache and satisfying the fantasies of overweight European tourists was much easier than keeping up with protected nesting spotted owls and the tree-hugging greeniacs moving into the Rockies from California and, worst of all, Portland.

Bob Davies prefers unreal life.

The dappled grey gelding's neck is arched like upholstery, its tail and mane are crimped. It stamps and paces, as if its heart will burst. Buffalo Bill is unsmiling under his handlebar mustache. He squints out at the audience. It's that thousand-yard stare. His horse stamps around a bit more, as if it could go crazy if it felt like it. But Buffalo Bill is heavy in his stirrups, deep in his seat.

"I brought some friends along tonight to meet you," Buffalo Bill says every night. "From the prairies and the Rocky Mountain states of Texas and Wyoming, Colorado and Montana," he says. "Raise the cover on your heads for my friends."

The cover on your heads?

Who has ever said that?

But the spectators get to their feet, and those with hats take them off.

A platinum-blond Annie Oakley in a long blue dress canters quickly into the arena on a very white horse, shooting the living dog out of everything she sees.

Pah! Pah!

There go Buffalo Bill's gloves, one at a time!

Annie Oakley whips a third pistol from beneath her skirts. *Pah! Pah! Pah!* She shoots a kettle and a pot from a Styrofoam rock next to the hologram of a campfire, then gallops offstage, firing off her pistols into the air, and hollering.

Buffalo Bill says, "You can't argue with that!"

The audience laughs.

"In an argument the woman always has the last word. Otherwise it's a new argument."

The audience laughs again. A drum rolls.

Buffalo Bill raises his right hand, like he's making a left turn on a bicycle. He says, "And now from the Great Plains of North America, allow me to introduce the stars of our show. The wise and the courageous, the only true Native Americans, the Indians." Buffalo Bill pauses. "Medicine Chief Sitting Bull," he says. "And his warrior braves."

The Mexican kid from Arizona who was supposed to be Medicine Chief Sitting Bull was found contemplating suicide on top of the roof of Le Carrousel de Lancelot his first night in France. He was sent home early. After that, the program director had to hire a disaffected French kid of Arab extraction from a rough neighborhood on the outskirts of the 18th arrondissement instead, and make him dye his long hair black.

"Welcome to you and your tribe, Medicine Chief Sitting Bull," Buffalo Bill from Sandpoint, Idaho, tells the disaffected French kid of Arab extraction. And then he says something

a real Wyoming Cowboy would be unlikely to say to an actual Red Man, and especially not a French kid of Arab extraction pretending to be a Red Man. "You honor us all with
your presence."

In the background meantime, Jerusalem and Daniel creep
up and down and around fake bluffs, like Indian scouts in a
1950s Western. They come into the arena and start to bob
about and make whooping noises. Their war bonnets are
unwieldy. Only the French kid of Arab extraction and Bob
Davies ride horses.

Afterward, the program manager says to the twins, "Please,
por favor, s'il vous plait, more energy. More sinister. You need
to pop off those rocks. Not this crawling about. You want my
opinion? You look like a couple of bored spiders. Wake up a
little bit. Maybe, you show me you're alive, I can put you on a
horse. Until then you are, yawn, yawn, yawn."

Jerusalem, Regained

There are more ways to lose a life than dying.

Daniel swinging from a lamppost, drunk.

He's kicking cars. His hoodie is bunched up around his shoulders.

He shouts at some gendarmes, "Hey, fuck you!"

"Let's head home," Jerusalem says.

Daniel takes a swing at his brother and misses. He staggers. "Fuckin'. Then they'll . . ." But Daniel is overtaken with the urge to vomit. "Oh, fuck."

Then he stands under a streetlight and wipes his mouth. His cheeks are hollow; there are blue shadows around his eyes. He's getting thin. He says, "Let's find somewhere open."

"Let's call it good, and go home," Jerusalem says.

"We got money, brah! The night is a child." Daniel laughs and flaps his hands around his face. "Let's find pussy."

Jerusalem catches Daniel by the feet and slams him to the ground. He sits on his back and quickly pulls his knife from his belt. He puts his knee across his brother's cheek and in one swipe of the blade he cuts off his brother's ponytail. Then he reaches behind his own neck, and makes another cut.

"When they ask you who died, you'll know what to tell them," Jerusalem says, standing up and closing the blade of his knife against his thigh. "Let's go. We're all done here."

The two black ponytails lie in the yellow glow cast by the streetlight.

(There Is No Such Thing as) The End

Once, when he was small, walking on a trail in the Black Hills with everyone, Jerusalem had noticed what appeared to be triangular pockets of mist in the branches of sun-bathed shrubs. But up close, the pockets of mist revealed themselves to be tiny tents. And in time those tents resolved into webs, and within those webs, when Jerusalem looked, there was the whirring activity of caterpillars frantically trying to seal themselves off from the world.

Their heads pulsed back and forth and back and forth as they tried to make a wall of silk between themselves and everything that was about to come next. As if they could. It looked so pointless to Jerusalem.

Le-a said, "Yeah. I bet we look pointless to them too. But one day, they'll fly. Imagine that."

Greenland

The man in the aisle seat was savaging bags of snacks. "I'm not nervous of flying," he said. "But I worry about many other things." He put a napkin over his mouth as he spoke. "The problem is, I like to be in control."

Daniel had closed his eyes.

"I'd feel better if I was flying this thing, honestly. Then at least, you know, I'm in control."

Jerusalem turned his face to the window.

For the first few hours, he watched the sun's glow ripen on the clouds, before they parted to reveal the Atlantic, impassive from this height, and immense.

"The sea, as far as you can see," Le-a used to tell Jerusalem when he asked what came after Turtle Island.

Which is how southern Greenland came as a surprise. For one thing, it's bigger than you'd think, and much whiter.

Jerusalem wondered what kind of people had learned how to live with all that snow and ice.

They'd be the sorts of people to respect solitude, he supposed. They'd know their precise and difficult place in that entire beautiful white expanse. They'd do everything as if their lives depended on it.

Everything.

The End

Every night when they were small, it was the same, Jerusalem remembered.

Rick Overlooking Horse prodded the fire. Then he lit his pipe and smoked quietly. Usually Le-a was asleep before the stories started. Squanto too. Rick Overlooking Horse said this time of night was for old people and children, the keepers of the wisdom. People in the middle of their years were busier, often doing unwise things, he said. They needed their sleep.

The inside of the old teepee glowed.

Rick Overlooking Horse began his wonderful, terrible tales of how the whole world came to be. And of how the Oglala Lakota Oyate came to be here now. He told the story of the White Buffalo Calf Woman, of the great warriors of the past, of the terrible battles to stay on the land.

When the stories grew wild, Jerusalem felt for Daniel's hand across the soft, tufty hide of the old buffalo bull.

"Tunkashila!" Daniel whispered when his alarm grew too much.

"How does it end?" Jerusalem needed to know. "Does it all end well?"

And then Rick Overlooking Horse's rough old hands touched the tops of their heads. "Oh yes," he said. "It ends well. It doesn't end soon, but it ends well. All of it."

6|17